AF593293

Nightmare

The *Nightmare* began when Roland John Raine defended George Bundock, criminal gang leader and sadist. Bundock went free, but Raine's wife went with him. Now Raine sits in St James's Park and runs over in his mind the steps he has taken to ensure that nobody will identify his own corpse. But the corpse was not to be Raine's. Sadie stayed on the edge of the *Nightmare*. She was a business lady with a good address in Shepherd Market, and she found herself with a minor body on her hands. Sadie was embarrassed, but luckily her hands were very experienced. Others were closer to the centre of the *Nightmare*: Eileen Prepend, of whom the description 'nymphomaniac' might be judged too coy; and Jacqueline, Raine's daughter, who worked among the methos of London's East End and in whose territory the other body was discovered. Arthur La Bern's new novel mixes murder with the twilight world of the mentally ill, as he asks who *are* the mentally sick and who the murderous sane.

By the same author

Fiction:

It Always Rains on Sunday
Night Darkens the Street
Paper Orchid
Pennygreen Street
It Was Christmas Every Day
The Big Money-Box
Brighton Belle
A Nice Class of People
It Will Be Warmer When It Snows
Goodbye Piccadilly, Farewell Leicester Square
Hallelujah!

Non-Fiction:

Life and Death of a Lady-Killer
Haigh: The Mind of a Murderer

Nightmare

Arthur La Bern

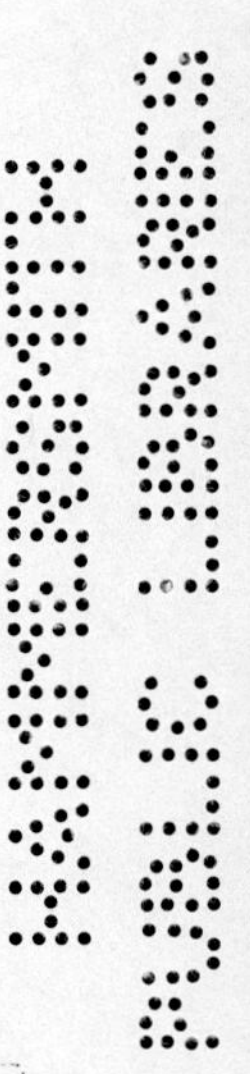

W. H. Allen · London
A division of Howard & Wyndham Ltd
1975

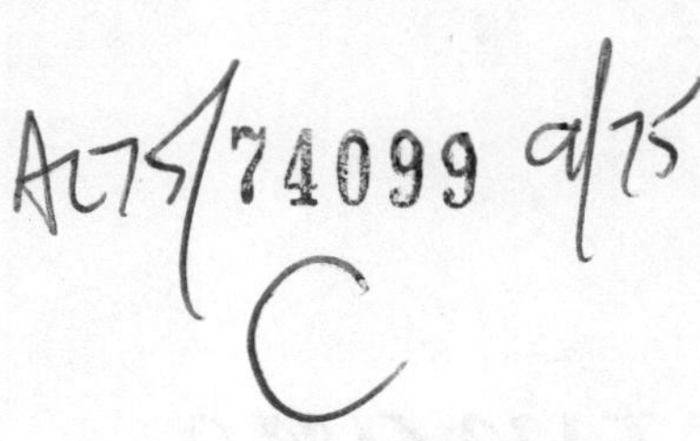

Printed in Great Britain by Northumberland Press Ltd, Gateshead
for the Publishers, W. H. Allen & Co. Ltd,
44 Hill Street, London W1X 8LB
Bound by Richard Clay (The Chaucer) Press Ltd, Bungay, Suffolk

ISBN 0 491 01733 2

Nightmare

I

THE LAST SOUNDS he heard before losing consciousness were the yakking of ducks, the honking of geese and the *rocoulement* of pigeons in St James's Park, the boom of Big Ben and the more distant but shriller rendition of time from a bugle on the square of Birdcage Walk barracks. Succumbing to the coma from which he did not anticipate recovering, it seemed—perversely—that his hearing in these few seconds had become more acute, as though all the sounds had emanated from his inner ear. Similarly, as his eyelids drooped on what should have been his last glimpse of life on earth, his vision became more vivid: colours were more brilliant, with flower beds taking on a shimmering, gossamer quality, trees becoming greener and the lake an almost South Seas blue. So much so that he experienced the hallucination of synaesthesia, believing that he could actually hear these colours. It was all rather pleasant. He felt no regret at the decision he had taken and implemented. He was aware only of a soothing euphoria.

Deep in a candy-striped deckchair, and having swallowed a massive dose of barbiturates washed down with half a pint of whisky, he could not think of a more pleasant place in which to die.

It was an easy way of death and he had taken care to ensure anonymity in his self-induced demise. He had removed the tailor's tag from his last suit, as well as the laundry and maker's tabs from his shirt. He was hatless and his shoes were not bespoke. He had destroyed all letters and documents. He had considered every unlikely event or incident that might foil his appointment with death. He had even thought of the improbability of some acquaintance happening along and stopping to chat. So, as his eyes began to close, he draped a newspaper across his face as if to shade himself from the midday sun.

Yet in considering the unlikely he had overlooked the likely. He overlooked the fact that there was a simple transaction involved in the hiring of a deck chair. He should have obtained a ticket for the chair before swallowing the pills.

When the man with a roll of tickets did arrive he thought that the recumbent occupant of the chair was one of those artful dodgers who attempt to avoid payment by feigning sleep. When this occupant of the chair failed to respond to the request for payment the ticket man lifted the newspaper from the sleeper's face. The face, chalk white, had lolled to one side, mouth open. The ticket man put his hand on the sleeper's shoulder.

'Mister.'

When this failed to elicit any response he rocked the chair gently. The motion, though slight, had a startling result. The occupant of the chair slithered on to the grass, and the impact of the fall did not awaken him.

It was then that the ticket man saw the empty whisky bottle and pillbox. He loped across the greenery, jumping a flower bed, coin bag swinging towards the park keepers' lodge. Then, seeing two constables sauntering along just outside the Park, he went off at a tangent, calling to them.

A few minutes later an ambulance, white harbinger of drama, blue lamp flashing, warning signal raucous enough to awaken the dead, had entered the main gates. As it arrived on the scene the policeman who had summoned it on his pocket radio was taking possession of the empty bottle and pillbox.

The blue-shirted ambulance men loaded their customer on to the foam rubber mattress with that minimum of effort which comes from long practice, pleased about the comparative simplicity of this open-air job. They tucked the blanket around him. One of the policemen took a seat alongside the unconscious man.

'Funny,' he murmured. 'I'm sure I know this face from somewhere.'

The doors closed. The ambulance bumped over grassy hillocks and asphalt paths towards the ornate, gold-leafed gates. The onlookers who had been attracted to this bonus *divertissement* returned to less dramatic pleasures, such as feeding inverted pyramids of sparrows on the little bridge spanning the lake, or victualling flotillas of mallards beneath.

The birds had long since nested when the failed suicide opened his eyes, then closed them wincingly as he realised to his chagrin that his bid had not come off, that he had been snatched from the valley of the shadow of death. He was conscious of two fingers on his wrist. He looked up. A West Indian nurse was studying her fob watch.

'Hullo,' she said. 'How you feeling?'

He shook his head. He was aware only of a feeling of humiliation. He was not in the least grateful.

'Would you like a cup of tea?'

'No, thank you. What hospital is this, please?'

'West End Central. Lucky for you it was so near.'

He realised that he had not been very clever. He should have chosen a more remote venue for his appointment with death. The old West End Central Hospital, long overdue for demolition, was less than half a mile from where he had attempted to close the door on his not unspectacular life. No, he had not been clever. He had been bloody inept.

He looked to left and right, realising that one of his wrists was attached to an intravenous drip. The ward, if so it could be described, was in a basement. Later he was to learn that it was unofficially known as the Odds and Sods Ward. It had once been used for storage of hospital equipment. Now it was used for storage of the human flotsam and jetsam picked up from the streets and open spaces of London. Here were the no-hopers, the drop-outs, the junkies and the hippies, every type of derelict except the meths drinkers—London's untouchables, the purple-visaged fraternity which rejected society as completely as they were themselves rejected. Only the French had a phrase for their condition—*nostalgie de la boue.*

The failed suicide's companions in this subterranean ward were only one remove from the methos, and did not look a great deal more prepossessing. They were all sitting up, watching a colour television that stood at the far end of the long room. They did not look like patients so much as visitants from another age and world, originals for the horror paintings of Bosch and Breughel. Despite their shoulder-length, ragged hair most of them were young, although there were a few oldsters. All seemed to have tattoo designs, either on their chests or arms, designs which they seemed proud to exhibit—those with tattooed sentiments on their arms had their pyjama sleeves rolled up to display them, and those with words and pictures on their chests had their pyjama jackets open. They were all as immobile as gargoyles on a medieval cathedral, all apparently entranced by the blood-shot eye of the filmy screen at the end of the ward. All wore headphones to receive the sound. Every now and then one of them would give vent to a Neanderthal grunt of appreciation.

The nurse was asking him for his name.

'I'm sorry,' he lied. 'I can't remember.'

'Oh, dear me.'

She knew he was lying and he knew she knew he was lying.

'That's awkward. What do we call you then? We've got to call you something. We can't say "Hey, you!", can we?'

'Why not? I don't mind.'

'Well, we do. It's not polite.'

'Just give me any old name, Adam, Shakespeare, Milton. I'll answer to it.'

'Don't you reckon it would be nicer if we knew your real name?'

'Maybe so, but as I can't remember it we'll have to make do with a substitute, won't we?'

'Is there any reason why you don't want to remember your name?'

'I can't imagine so.'

'You took a mighty big overdose, didn't you?'

'I suppose I did.'

'You remember that, but you don't remember your name? Come on now!'

He could not but help admire her. She had set a little verbal trap for him and he had fallen into it. She was smiling at him and he smiled back, but he wasn't falling for any more of her tender verbal traps.

'I'm sorry, nurse, but there it is.'

At this moment a young doctor arrived at his bedside. Hands in grey flannel trousers, a clipboard under his arm, stethoscope around his neck, pens clipped to the pocket of his white coat, a lock of fair hair falling over one of his English blue eyes, he announced himself as Dr Maynard. The nurse began to pull the curtains around the bed.

Dr Maynard reached for the bedside chair and sat astride it, arms folded on the back of it as he faced the patient.

'And how are we?'

'Possibly better than I deserve to be.'

'Why do you say that?'

'I'm told I took a mighty big overdose.'

'You did indeed.'

The young doctor was unscrewing the cap of his fountain pen, blue eyes smiling into the darker eyes of the man he had brought back from the dead.

'I don't appear to have your name,' he said.

The observation was as casual as if it implied some oversight on his own part or that of the nursing staff.

'As a matter of fact I was just telling nurse I couldn't remember it.'

Dr Maynard did not appear to be in the least put out, but his mouth puckered.

'That's a bit of a bind, isn't it?'

'Yes, I suppose it is. I'm sorry.'

'So am I.'

The man in the bed felt just a bit curmudgeonly. Dr Maynard was such a likeable young chap and had been instrumental in saving his life. He was not grateful to him for that, but he did not wish to be ungracious.

'Well, as you can't remember your name, I suppose we'll have to put you down as Mr A. N. Other. Ever played cricket?'

'I have a vague recollection of the game.'

'Did you play?'

'Why do you ask?'

'It just occurred to me you might have been a stone-walling type of batsman.'

Dr Maynard stood up, clipping his stethoscope to his ear.

'I'd like to listen to your ticker.'

The patient bared his chest. The doctor listened.

'Take a deep breath.'

He did so.

'And again.'

He took another deep breath.

'Again. Good, good. Now say ninety-nine. Good.'

Dr Maynard reached for the chart.

'By the way, how are the waterworks?'

'I haven't tested them here, but as far as I can recollect they were in running order.'

'A good flow?'

'A good flow. Why do you ask?'

'We took a blood sample and found a very high level of alcohol.'

Dr Maynard was putting the stethoscope into the largest of the pockets on his white coat.

'Where did you obtain all those barbiturates?'

'I saved them up.'

'So you had been planning this attempt for some time?'

'I suppose so.'

'For how long?'

'Six months, maybe longer.'

'You remember that, but you don't remember your name?'

'Look, Dr Maynard, I thought we'd agreed that my name was A. N. Other? I'm quite happy with that. After all, I am just another patient.'

'There is no such animal as just another patient. Why are you so anxious to conceal your identity?'

'Why do you ask?'

'Because we noticed that you had cut the tailor's tag from the inside of your suit, and it certainly wasn't a suit off the peg.'

'Doctor, all I wanted to do was to get off the peg myself.'

He had no desire to be helpful but he realised that if he answered one question it would only lead to another. Give his name and then they'd want to know the name of his next of kin. Give them that and then they'd inform Veronica and she'd preen herself that he had made the attempt on his life because of her—which was only partly true—and he had no desire to give her the satisfaction of acting out the role of a *femme fatale*.

Dr Maynard was clipping his pen back. He smiled somewhat ruefully, smothered the incipient yawn that comes from a long day's work and said, 'Ah, well. There will be a hot drink coming round shortly. Perhaps it will help revive your memory.'

'Thank you, doctor. I'm sorry I wasn't more helpful.'

The young doctor shrugged and walked away, combing his hair with his fingers in a gesture of frustration. The failed suicide felt almost sorry for the man who had saved his life.

* * *

The hot drinks came round on a trolley and the television was switched off. Simultaneously, the night sister arrived at his bedside. She was broad-hipped and appropriately bosomed, her rank shown in her distinctive head-dress as well as by the silver badge on her belt. She had carroty hair and not unpleasing freckles.

'You missed supper, didn't you?'

'I suppose I did. It didn't occur to me.'

'I'll get you something from the kitchen.'

'Please, Sister. I'd rather you didn't.'

'But you must eat.'

'I'd rather not.'

He also declined the hot drink. The lights were switched off. He sat up in bed, hands clasped behind his neck, staring into space, wondering what the outcome would be, furious with himself for making a botch of things. Eventually, he must have dozed. In the small hours he awakened to a sound of scuffling on the ventilator shaft which ran the entire length of the ward. Sliding a pillow from beneath him, he hurled it at the scurrying creatures.

The night sister appeared, hushing and tushing, followed by a nurse.

'What is it?'

'Sister, this place is alive with rats.'

'Nonsense, you're just seeing things.'

'You're right. I am seeing things. Rats. Don't tell me I've got dee-tees, because I haven't. I saw them on that ventilator shaft. That's why I threw my pillow.'

'I'm not saying you've got dee-tees,' she whispered soothingly. 'But people can imagine all sorts of things at night in this old place. I know I do.'

The nurse had retrieved his pillow. The night sister took it from her.

'Let me make those pillows more comfortable,' she said.

The elbow of her plump, freckled arm went round his neck. To his surprise, he found the aseptic odour of her body and the starched uniform stimulating, particularly when a wisp of her reddish hair brushed across his cheek as she stacked the pillows.

'There, is that more comfy?'

It was and he told her so, apologising for the disturbance but assuring her that he really had seen those rats. She asked him if he wouldn't like a cup of tea and some biscuits perhaps. He said he would if she brought them herself. She said she would do her best, but first she had to do the round of the female equivalent of the Odds and Sods ward. She didn't tell him, but unofficially it was known as the Whores and Sores Ward.

The failed suicide was asleep again when the night sister brought the tea and biscuits. So she put them on the bedside table, placing the saucer on top of the cup.

When next he opened his eyes the day staff was coming on duty. The saucer was still on top of the cup of cold tea and he gazed uncomprehendingly at the plate on which there was nothing but a few biscuit crumbs. Then he sat up and called to the nearest nurse.

'Nurse, would you mind bringing me my clothes?'

Staff Nurse Frimley wore squarish, rimless spectacles. She was that type, but she was pretty like a Meissen figurine and equally cold.

She ignored his request and put a thermometer into his mouth, reaching for his wrist and looking at her watch all in one movement. Having taken temperature and pulse, she reached for the chart on the bed rail.

'Why is there no name on this chart?'

'Because I didn't give my name.'

'But you cannot refuse to give your name.'

'Why not?'

'For one thing it isn't polite.'

'You have a point there.'

'Then may I have your name now, please?'

He said he was sorry, but he could not give it. This didn't please Staff Nurse Frimley one little bit.

'I've never heard such nonsense,' she snapped. 'Who do you think you are? A pop star, a film star, a Cabinet Minister that you can ride roughshod over the rules?'

'I'm glad you have your sense of protocol right, but I don't want to ride roughshod over any rules. All I want to do is to get out of this place.'

'It was your own action that got you into this place, as you choose to call it.'

She really was a spitfire, was Staff Nurse Frimley. Yet he could not help but admire her. He watched her writing some figures on the chart, left-handed. He had always been fascinated by left-handed women. Veronica was left-handed, the bitch.

'I admit that,' he said. 'And I have apologised for the trouble I have caused. I wish to cause no further trouble and I would like to leave. So please may I have my clothes?'

'I have no authority to send for your clothes. Yes or no?'

He was puzzled by the cryptic question.

'Yes or no what?'

'Have you had your bowels open?'

'No.'

She replaced the chart and proceeded to the next bed. He contemplated getting out of bed and making a dash for the nearest exit, clad in the hospital pyjamas, but gave up the idea as not feasible even in permissive London of the day.

He declined breakfast, but said he would like to have a bath. He felt like a cur that had rolled over and over in some unpleasant substance. He felt as if he had crawled from beneath stones, leaving a slimy trail. He felt as if he had been swimming in a sewer and swallowed his own vomit.

He also said he would like to have a shave and then decided against it. The West Indian nurse re-assured him—the electric razor was sterilised every time it was used.

It was the West Indian nurse who accompanied him to the bathroom in the corridor. She had given him a zebra-crossing striped bathrobe and a pair of down-at-heel slippers which were clammy to the feet.

She showed him the plug for the electric razor and then turned on both taps of the bath, which stood on pedestals and was mottled with spinach-hued stains. While he shaved, she sat on the edge of the bath, watching it fill and testing the temperature.

Having shaved, he took off the pyjama jacket which was too skimpy to button across his chest.

'Thanks,' he said, waiting for her to go. 'I can manage.'

The nurse got up from the edge of the bath and took a seat on the Windsor-type chair.

'Sure,' she said. 'You go ahead.'

Only now did he realise that he wasn't to be allowed to have a bath in privacy in case he drowned himself in the bath or hanged himself from one of the pipes. It seemed he was to be under permanent surveillance. Deciding to make the best of it, he took his bath in about as much time as it takes to run the Gimcrack Stakes.

When he got back to the Odds and Sods Ward he saw that Dr Maynard was on his morning round with Staff Nurse Frimley. The young doctor greeted him with a genial quip.

'And how's our man of mystery this morning?'

The patient was in no mood for such pleasantries. He told the doctor that he had never been so humiliated in his life. The doctor looked genuinely surprised, flicking back that recalcitrant lock of fair hair.

'Really? In what way?'

'I do prefer to take a bath in privacy, you know.'

Dr Maynard laughed.

'Oh, come, come, old chap. Lots of fellows would love to take a bath with a pretty nurse around. But seriously, it's a precaution we have to take. Supposing you'd slipped on a piece of soap and cut your head open?'

'I've been taking unaided baths all my adolescent and adult life and I've never yet slipped on a piece of soap.'

'Then let me be more blunt. Supposing you'd decided to keep your head under the bath water?—then I'd be in hot water too, wouldn't I?'

The doctor laughed at his own joke, laughter in which the patient did not join.

'Now,' said Dr Maynard. 'If you like to pop back on to the bed I'll have a look and a listen at you.'

'Really, doctor,' he protested. 'Do we have to go through this routine all over again? There's nothing wrong with me.'

Staff Nurse Frimley was pulling the curtains around the bed and the patient had a sudden unreasonable intuition that she and the doctor were lovers. He felt an equally unreasonable stab of jealousy.

'It won't take long,' said Dr Maynard.

Once more he applied his stethoscope. Then he tapped him all over with his knuckles, scratched the soles of his feet, shone a torch into his eyes, inspected his finger nails and appeared to be generally satisfied.

'All things considered, you're in pretty good shape. All things considered.'

'All things considered, may I now have my clothes, so that I can leave?'

'I'd like you to see our psycho' first.'

'Dr Maynard, are you suggesting that I am out of my mind?'

'Good Lord no, but in all cases of attempted suicide we have to call in the psycho'. Nothing to worry about, just a formality.'

'It's a formality I prefer to dispense with.'

Dr Maynard smiled and shrugged before passing on to the next bed.

'I'm sorry,' he said. 'But that's the drill.'

Twenty-five minutes later Dr Emrys Shiplake came on the scene. He was obviously far more important than young Dr Maynard. He was older and, as a mark of his own self-esteem, he did not wear a white coat, being attired in well-cut clerical grey, side vents on the jacket and four buttons on each sleeve. A thin gold watch chain was suspended across his waistcoat. His white shirt showed plenty of cuff and the links were of onyx. He wore black half-brogues and black silk socks.

As soon as the failed suicide saw Dr Shiplake approaching the bed he knew that all his efforts to conceal his name had been futile. This smooth gentleman knew him. They had met before in somewhat different circumstances.

Dr Emrys Shiplake, consultant psychiatrist to the Inner London Hospital Group, had been witness for the defence in a case at the Old Bailey where he—Roland John Raine—had been counsel for the prosecution. It had been Roland Raine's task to demolish the expert evidence of Dr Shiplake and he had done so with a relish and panache that old-timers said was reminiscent of the great F. E. Smith himself. He had made the learned doctor look and sound like a Tony Lumpkin in the witness box.

'Hello, Raine,' said Dr Shiplake. 'What brings you here?'

'Surely you know.'

'Oh, I did hear something about an overdose. All too common these days, I'm afraid. But tell me, Raine, why? Why did you do it?'

'It's a long story.'

'I'm prepared to listen.'

Dr Shiplake sat on the bedside chair, taking a thin gold pencil from his waistcoat pocket and a small notebook from his hip.

'Now, let's have chapter and verse, shall we?'

'I'd rather not. It's all rather personal.'

'Of course it's all rather personal. People don't try to do themselves in unless it is rather personal. That's why I'm here. To help you sort it out.'

'I don't want to sort it out.'

Dr Shiplake put his right ankle on his left knee, showing plenty of sock. He appeared to be studying his shoelace.

'I'm only here to help.'

'I don't want any help.'

'Any person who attempts to take his own life needs help.'

'In my case, no.'

'You seem most adamant.'

'Perhaps that is my nature.'

'You know, Raine, in the few minutes we've been talking here you could have told me what drove you to take this decision.'

'I wasn't driven to it. I arrived at the decision by a process of reasoning. I came to the conclusion that I did not wish to go on living. It's as simple as that.'

'I'm sure it was far from simple. Couldn't you just give me an inkling?'

'I'll give you a résumé then. My wife ran off with a client. Then my young daughter, feeling unwanted I presume, left home on some crazy project of trying to rehabilitate meths drinkers, of all people. I took increasingly to the whisky bottle—as the drinks got more frequent the briefs got fewer and fewer. I have not had a brief in the last two years and I doubt whether another one would ever come my way—not even if the entire criminal bar was struck down by cholera. So I decided to end it. That's the story in a nutshell.'

Dr Emrys Shiplake had made a few notes in his little book.

'So that's the story in a nutshell. Now, shall we have the kernel of it. With whom did your wife run off'

'I told you—a client. A man I'd defended at the Old Bailey.'

'Yes, but can't we be a little more specific? What sort of man?'

'He was a villain—a gangster.'

'When you defended him at the Old Bailey what was the indictment?'

'Extortion, demanding money with menaces, conspiring to defeat the ends of justice. The Crown had thrown the book at him.'

'And you threw it back?'

'I got a Not Guilty verdict, if that's what you mean.'

'That was quite a feat on your part?'

'I wouldn't claim all the credit—if credit it can be called. The prosecution witnesses were terrified.'

'Terrified of what?'

'Reprisals. But I don't see what all this has got to do with the present.'

'I'm coming to that. When you speak of reprisals—who would have carried out the reprisals.'

'Bundock's associates—if he went down.'

'Bundock was the man your wife ran off with?'

'That is so.'

'But were not Bundock's associates in the dock with him?'

'There isn't a dock large enough to accommodate all Bundock's associates.'

'I see.'

Dr Shiplake twirled the thin gold pencil between pink, immaculate fingers, looking down at it reflectively. Raine began to wonder whether he would dangle it before his eyes like a metronome.

'How did your wife meet this Mr Bundock?'

'At the celebration party he threw after his acquittal. It was foolish of me to go to it—and even more foolish to take Veronica.'

'Why did you?'

'Because Veronica asked me to do so.'

'Did you usually do everything your wife asked you to do?'

'I think so, yes.'

Dr Shiplake nodded, now twirling the thin gold pencil in the opposite direction, pursing his lips as though he was about to arrive at a momentous conclusion.

'Even if the request was unreasonable?'

'I have no recollection of her ever making an unreasonable request.'

'You would not consider that a request for you—an eminent Queen's Counsel—to take her to a gangster's party ... unreasonable?'

'I did not think so at the time. We went most places together.'

'Even to gangster's parties?'

'This was the first—and only—occasion. I've already said it was foolish. It was a blunder of the first magnitude.'

Raine was beginning to feel more than a little rankled. The bedside interview was becoming inquisitorial, if not impertinent and, as far as he could see, it served no useful purpose.

'And I would like to add this, Dr Shiplake. I do not see the point of this interminable question-and-answer routine about matters that are strictly personal. It was for this very reason that I did not give my name to the staff here, because I realised that answering one question would lead to others. I wished to avoid publicity.'

'The hospital was scarcely likely to send out a press release about you,' the doctor replied drily.

'Perhaps not, but unfortunate happenings like mine have a habit of leaking into the newspapers. I can imagine the headlines.'

'It would not be the first time you had been in the headlines?'

'Any publicity I received in the past was strictly confined to my professional activities.'

'Supposing that your bid for self-destruction had succeeded—would it have mattered if it had been headlined?'

'Not to me, perhaps, but it might have been upsetting to people who were once my friends.'

'Ah! Now we might be getting somewhere. Do you imagine that you have no friends?'

'I did not say that, Dr Shiplake. I had a wide circle of friends. It is I who have avoided them—not the other way about.'

'You preferred to be alone in your misery?'

'Since you put it like that—yes.'

'Good. I'm so glad we agree on something at last. Tell me, Raine, has there been any insanity in your family?'

'There has not.'

'None of your forebears ever attempted suicide?'

'I don't like the implication, Dr Shiplake. You link suicidal tendencies with insanity.'

'You haven't answered my question.'

'All right, I'll answer it. None of my forebears, as far as I know, ever attempted suicide. For the love of Christ! Where is all this getting us?'

'To an understanding perhaps. Now tell me—'

'Dr Shiplake, if you want me to answer any more questions—do you mind if we have the curtains drawn?'

The psychiatrist looked mildly surprised, as if it were some eccentric request on the patient's part.

'Oh, does it worry you? By all means then.'

'It doesn't worry me,' said Raine. 'But it seems a trifle illogical that in a hospital where the curtains are pulled whenever a patient has his hands and face washed, that same patient is expected to elaborate on the most intimate facts of his life in the full view and hearing of everybody else in the ward.'

'I'm sorry,' said Dr Shiplake. 'I didn't realise that a chap like you, accustomed to the cut and thrust of the courts, would be so self-conscious. I don't believe anybody is eavesdropping. However.'

He twisted around in the chair and asked a nurse to draw the curtains. So, the *eminence gris*, the great psycho', couldn't deign to draw the curtains himself. To Raine it seemed as if he was indicating that he, Dr Emrys Shiplake, did not draw curtains over life. He uncovered, he lifted veils, made everything crystal clear, simplified all that appeared complex and solved that which appeared insoluble, stripping life down to its essentials, the veneer from the panelling. The curtains were drawn.

'This man Bundock, presumably he had a wife. What happened to her? When he went off with your wife?'

'I presume he paid her off. Perhaps she went back to whoring. That's how she started.'

'And what was your wife before you married her?'

Raine wasn't sure that he approved of the juxtaposition of the questions, but put it down to the doctor's lack of finesse rather than to any malice aforethought.

'She was an actress.'

'A good actress?'

'She was the youngest student ever to win the RADA gold medal.'

'And she was successful?'

'She was in a West End play when we met.'

'Would I know her stage name?'

'She was Veronica Lund.'

'A star?'

'She would have been if she had not given up the stage to marry me.'

'At your request?'

'No, she was going to have our child, Jacqueline.'

'So you had intercourse before you married?'

'Yes, but I don't see what—'

'Was she a virgin when you met her?'

'How many girls of twenty are virgins these days—or were, even in those days?'

'You mean she had slept around a bit?'

'Dr Shiplake, I think you're being quite offensive.'

'I'm sorry. I apologise, Raine. I did not intend to be. I'm trying to help you and the fact that you so suddenly lose your temper indicates that we might be nearing the cause of the trouble. In psychiatry, a certain amount of probing is as necessary as in surgery.'

'I did not "suddenly" lose my temper, Dr Shiplake. It has been simmering for the past twenty minutes.'

'Raine, I once heard you tell a witness in Court that there was no need for him to lose his temper.'

'I was wondering when you would get around to that. The difference is that I am not in a witness box. I'm in a hospital bed, in not very congenial surroundings and with the dregs of humanity on all sides.'

'Yes, I do sympathise with you there, Raine,' said Dr Shiplake with a sudden unexpected show of concern. 'It's not the most salubrious ward in London, I admit. However, we'll get you out of it as soon as we can.'

The last observation cheered Raine. He would put up with the psycho's impertinent questioning for a little longer if it resulted in his discharge from this subterranean limbo.

Dr Shiplake was studying the notes he had made, nodding to himself as if in satisfaction, pleased with the results of his line of questioning.

'Now, Raine. Would you say that your wife and you were mutually satisfying partners, sexually?'

'I was wondering when you would get around to the sex bit, too. Yes, I would say that we were. It so happens that is one of the reasons why we got married.'

'Your wife was quite satisfied with you in bed?'

'Yes.'

'How do you know?'

'I just happen to know.'

'How do you know?'

'How do I know? What do you want me to say—describe her orgasms?'

'Raine, old chap. There is no need to shout.'

'Is there any need for these questions?'

Dr Shiplake leaned forward and put his elbows on the side of the bed, twirling the thin gold pencil between his fingers.

'Yes, there is,' he said. 'Your wife was an actress. Is it not possible that she simulated satisfaction when she was in bed with you?'

Raine's first reaction was to hit him, and he would have done so but for the fact that one wrist was attached to an intravenous drip.

Shiplake, he knew, was being deliberately offensive. He was goading him as he—Raine—would not have goaded even the most recalcitrant witness. Yet it could be argued that the doctor was acting quite properly within his terms of reference. To a psychiatrist nothing is sacred.

To Raine, psychiatry was so much pseudo scientific claptrap. He had to face the disagreeable fact, however, that his release from this *cul de basse fosse* was very much in the pink hands of the highly respected Dr Emrys Shiplake.

He leaned as far forward as the drip attachment would permit and said, 'Dr Shiplake, I think you're on to something I didn't realise before.'

'Oh, yes. What is that?'

'It only occurs to me now that my wife did simulate satisfaction in bed. Every time we had intercourse she recited the balcony scene from *Romeo and Juliet*.'

'Now you're just being flippant, Raine. It seems to me that you are avoiding answering the question.'

'A distasteful question savouring of voyeurism.'

'All right. If you find the question distasteful, let us try another line. Why did you take it so badly when your wife left you?'

'Well, she was my wife.'

'Agreed, but lots of men's wives run off with other men, and they don't all attempt to take their lives as a consequence.'

'Remember that I'd lost my daughter too. I loved them both. They were my whole life.'

'Yet they both deserted you.'

'I don't think my daughter deserted me. I think she was so

shocked by her mother's defection that she felt rejected herself and went into this idealistic trauma in which she imagined she could help the most rejected of all society's rejects.'

'That's a likely theory, but why do you suppose she decided on trying to help meths drinkers rather than, say, lepers, thalidomide or autistic children?'

'Possibly because she thought too few people had attempted to help those who refused to help themselves. I think she'd read a book about it by another barrister's daughter.'

'Have you instituted divorce proceedings?'

'No.'

'Why not? Are you hoping that your wife will come back to you?'

'I would scarcely have attempted to take my own life if I'd entertained any hopes in that direction.'

A rattle of crockery was heard from behind the curtaining and Staff Nurse Frimley asked if they would like coffee.

The coffee was not recognisable as such, but it was welcome as a respite and Staff Nurse Frimley actually smiled at him, called him 'Mr Raine'. Now that he was no longer anonymous it appeared that he had gained in status.

'You were about to tell me why you did not institute divorce proceedings,' said Shiplake.

'Can't you imagine the headlines? "Q.C.'s Wife Ran Off With Gangster." '

The doctor twirled the thin gold pencil and made another note.

'It does occur to me that you have an outsize phobia about adverse publicity. I get the impression that your pride was more wounded than your heart. Would you have felt so bad about it if your wife had gone off with—let us say, another barrister?'

'How would you feel if your wife went off with a hospital porter?'

'I am not married.'

So, thought Raine, here I am being subjected to a distasteful, tactless and embarrassing interrogation about my marriage by a man who isn't even married himself. Some woman somewhere was probably counting her lucky stars. He wondered whether male psychiatrists ever married female psychiatrists.

'When you say you hit the bottle, how much were you drinking a day?'

'At one point I got up to three bottles a day.'

Dr Shiplake shook his head very slowly, looking at Raine as if trying to fathom how he could have possibly survived.

'That's a lot of whisky.'

'It is. It took a lot of money too. To buy the last few bottles I sold my wig.'

'I wouldn't have thought that a barrister's second-hand wig would have had much market value.'

'On the contrary, my wig was genuine horse-hair. Most of the wigs made today are nylon. Besides, my wig had a well-worn look about it. Young barrister's don't like new wigs. They like to give the impression that they are old hands.'

'That's very interesting. It does suggest that members of your profession are inclined to show off?'

'I don't think so. It is just that young men starting out on a career don't like to look immature—the same applies to all professions.'

'How did you go about selling your wig?'

'I took it to Ravenscroft's.'

'One final question, Raine. Supposing we discharge you from this hospital ... are you likely to contemplate having another go at yourself?'

'At the moment I cannot answer that truthfully, because I just don't know.'

Dr Emrys Shiplake stood up, closing his notebook and replacing the thin gold pencil. He shot his cuffs, the gesture of a man who had just come to a decision.

'The first thing to do is to get you out of here,' he said.

Raine's heart almost warmed to him. Perhaps he wasn't such a bad fellow, after all. Raine had been wrong to read voyeuristic or even more unworthy motives into his questioning, embarrassing though it had been.

'Thank you, doctor,' he said. 'How soon?'

'As soon as possible,' Dr Shiplake replied.

The curtains parted. The doctor departed. A nurse pulled the curtaining back, so that the ward, this *corde sanitaire* of human derelicts and drop-outs, was once more visible. Looking down the entire length of it, Raine noticed for the first time that there was not so much as one small bunch of flowers on any of the bedside tables. The most forlorn graveyards have a few withered blooms in a jam jar, but here there was not a petal for the living dead. Here there were no visiting hours, because nobody bothered to visit.

The trolley with the midday meal was coming round, although it was not yet noon. The other inmates were sitting up eagerly, saliva-eager, drooling anticipation.

'Soup, Mr Raine?'

'No, thanks.'

'Fish cakes and cabbage?'

'No, thank you, nurse.'

Staff Nurse Frimley walked over to his bed, her square glasses glinting, then stood looking at him, arms folded over her starched bosom.

'Mr Raine, you really should eat, you know. You've had nothing since you came in here. Nothing but a couple of biscuits in the night.'

'I didn't have the biscuits, Staff Nurse.'

'You must have eaten them in your sleep then. Sister McFarlane said she put some biscuits on your bedside table with a cup of tea at three o'clock this morning.'

'I saw only the crumbs on the plate and some crumbs on the floor.'

'Are you suggesting that one of the other patients had the biscuits?'

'No, but I do suggest you call in the rodent officer.'

He realised he was getting on the wrong side of Staff Nurse Frimley again. There was no point in it. It was no concern of his that the place was rat-infested. It didn't seem to worry the other patients.

'I don't understand what you're talking about, Mr Raine,' said Staff Nurse Frimley.

Raine felt enormous respect for her. Here was this skilled young woman, working in conditions that would have appalled a Florence Nightingale, tending as unsavoury a collection of *clochards* as he had seen outside Paris or anywhere else for that matter, going coolly about her duties with crisp efficiency, undeterred by the proximity of a most loathsome form of vermin life and even carrying off a convincing pretence that it was not there.

'No,' he said. 'I must have been seeing things in the night.'

'Yes, Mr Raine, I believe you must have been seeing things in the night. Now, what about some lunch? We can't allow you leave without having a meal.'

So she had already heard on the grapevine that he was going to be discharged. That made it official. He felt so grateful that he was almost tempted to try the lunch, but his courage evaporated when he saw the pink sauce being ladled on to the fishcakes and caught a whiff of the cabbage water.

'I really don't think I could manage it, Staff Nurse,' he said. 'And it would be such a pity to waste good food.'

Staff Nurse Frimley smiled and the trolley moved on. The next-bed neighbour to Raine was wiping driblets of pink sauce off his chin with the cuff of his pyjama sleeve and demanding, 'What's for afters?'

There was really no reason for Raine to be so elated at the prospect of his release. He had no money and nowhere to go. Neither had he the resolution as yet to make a second attempt on his life and he was not quite sure, thinking about it, that he wished to do so. It was almost twenty-four hours since he had swallowed those barbiturates and, miraculously, he was still alive. Whether it was a reason for rejoicing was another matter.

He might well have said, with Swinburne, that he was weary of days and hours, blown buds of barren flowers, desires and dreams and powers and everything but sleep where life has death for neighbour. But he would have preferred to liken death to a mistress rather than a neighbour, a mistress in whose arms one found eternal oblivion. Yesterday he'd been dragged from her arms.

This morbid reverie was broken by the approach of a girl uncommonly pretty. When a man is still susceptible to feminine allure he does not really desire death. She wore a white coat and at first he thought she was a woman doctor. He was wrong.

'Good morning, Mr Raine. My name is Vanessa Jordan. I'm Dr Shiplake's secretary.'

Lucky Shiplake.

'Good morning, Miss Jordan. What good news have you for me?'

'Dr Shiplake has asked me to tell you that he has made arrangements for you to be transferred to another hospital—a hospital in the country where you will receive suitable treatment.'

'I'm sorry, I didn't quite hear that.'

She touched her auburn curls and her greenish-grey eyes flicked with the merest suggestion of petulance.

'I said that Dr Shiplake has asked me to tell you that he has made arrangements for you to be transferred to another hospital.'

'Oh, and what hospital is that?'

'Brinstead Manor. It's a much nicer hospital than this—it's out in the country, you know.'

'I know,' he said. 'I know all about Brinstead Manor Hospital, thank you.'

He flung the sheets back and swung his legs out of bed, reaching for the zebra-crossing dressing gown, unmindful of the fact that he was attached to a saline drip, so that the entire paraphernalia came crashing to the floor.

Staff Nurse Frimley entered, running.

'Mr Raine, what on earth is the matter?'

'Never mind, just bring me my clothes—or I'll walk out of here as I am.'

He was reaching under the bed for the clammy slippers. Miss Vanessa Jordan went off at a trot, pearly thumb-nails protruding from the pockets of her white coat which was not long enough to conceal her shapely legs. Obviously she was off to acquaint Dr Shiplake with the latest development.

'Mr Raine,' Staff Nurse Frimley pleaded. 'You know I have no authorisation to bring you your clothes and you cannot walk out of here dressed as you are.'

'Why not? Am I a prisoner?'

'Of course not, Mr Raine, but you are a patient and as such you are our responsibility.'

'A responsibility that you are now delegating to Brinstead Manor Hospital. No, thank you! No, thank you!'

'Why do you object to going to Brinstead Manor, Mr Raine?'

'Because I happen to know that Brinstead Manor is a mental hospital with just about the worst reputation in the country, its locked wards full of recidivists.'

'Mr Raine, all I know is that it is a psychiatric hospital with a considerable reputation.'

'A reputation for brutality and sadism, both physical and mental, allied to medical supervision of such abysmally low standard that it would not be tolerated even in one of Her Majesty's Prisons.'

'How did you come to form this opinion about Brinstead, Mr Raine?'

Raine told her. He told her what some of his clients had told him. They would prefer to do five years on the Moor than six months in Brinstead. She retorted that if he chose to believe the assertions of criminals then that was his affair. He could have slapped her face.

Miss Vanessa Jordan came back into the ward and called Staff Nurse Frimley aside. Raine could not hear what they were saying but he guessed that their brief conversation was centred upon himself.

He stretched out on top of the bed, staring at the ventilator shaft, pursing his lips over clenched teeth, trying to figure out what to do, trying to restrain himself from going berserk, going in search of Dr Emrys Shiplake and knocking him flat. He closed his eyes and began silently to count up to a hundred.

When he opened his eyes again he saw Staff Nurse Frimley at his bedside. She was holding a hypodermic needle. She told him that Dr Shiplake had asked her to administer a sedative.

'A sedative for what?'

'To calm you down for the journey. You must admit that you are a trifle overwrought. You were grinding your teeth just now.'

'Staff Nurse Frimley, I'm sorry, but I refuse. What you euphemistically describe as a sedative is a shot to put me out so that I will not be able to resist being carried off to a loony bin.'

'Please, Mr Raine, don't make it difficult for both of us. I have my job to do. You are a sick man. Any decisions that are taken are in your own interests.'

'That be damned for a tale,' he retorted.

He got up off the bed and would have walked out of the ward towards the street, but found his way barred by two young porters in blue serge uniforms as bulky as themselves. One was Spanish, the other Irish, both with mops of shaggy black hair. 'Would you mind?' Raine asked. 'You're in my way.'

The porters would not budge.

'Staff Nurse Frimley, would you mind asking these young men to get out of my way?'

'I'm sorry, Mr Raine, you cannot leave.'

'You intend keeping me here by force?'

'No, you are being transferred to Brinstead Manor.'

'Forcibly?'

'Mr Raine, will you please come back to bed and take this sedative? You either submit to it willingly or I will have to resort to the assistance of the porters.'

Raine could not quite believe his ears or his eyes. This was London, England, not Moscow, not Warsaw, not Athens, not Barcelona, not Prague.

He eyed the impassive-faced, black-haired porters. He knew there was no point in resisting. It would all be too undignified. It was a question of the lesser of two gross indignities.

He turned and went back to the bed.

'All right, Staff Nurse Frimley. You win. Go ahead, but I want to make it quite clear that I submit to this under duress. And as soon as I have the opportunity I shall play hell about it.'

'Just relax on the bed,' she said soothingly, 'and pull down the tops of your pyjama legs.'

She was holding the hypodermic needle up to the light. She did not draw the curtains and the two porters had moved in close to the bed as if anticipating trouble. He rolled over, face downwards, pulling down his pyjama legs.

He felt Staff Nurse Frimley's fingers inside the pyjamas, pulling them down even further so that his entire buttocks were now on display.

'Which side would you like it in?'

'Oh, take your pick.'

'I think the left one is a little plumper,' she said.

'Help yourself.'

She dabbed at his rump with a piece of wet cotton wool. Then, less than a second later, he felt the cold bite of the needle. It seemed to be penetrating by at least six inches and it was as much as he could do to prevent himself squirming. Then came another dab of damp cotton wool and a brisk, circular rubbing of it.

'There,' said Staff Nurse Frimley. 'That wasn't so bad, was it?'

Her voice sounded a long, long way off. The bed was beginning to revolve in slow motion. She pulled his pyjama legs up and gave his bottom a pat.

When he recovered consciousness, Raine saw that on the bedside chair there was a pillow case containing his clothes: suit, shirt, pants, socks, tie and shoes all bundled in together. The West Indian nurse came and took them out. They looked woefully crumpled. She also asked if he would like a cup of tea. He said he would, but when she brought it he couldn't drink it. She offered to help him dress and he declined, saying he could manage, but he couldn't. He just hadn't got the strength.

'I'd let the nurse help, if I were you, old chap.'

There was a stranger at the bedside. A tall, round-shouldered man with a toothy, benign expression. He wore a pin-stripe suit in Burton blue, the effect of a white handkerchief jutting from his breast pocket being somewhat marred by the bowl of a pipe and the clips of various ballpoint pens.

'Good a'ternoon,' the stranger said. 'I am the Inner London Council's Mental Health Officer.'

'Say that again,' said Raine.

The stranger repeated his introduction. Raine still did not quite comprehend, feeling comatose, weak as a rag doll, finding his fingers all thumbs as he tried to button up the flies of his crumpled trousers. The nurse was tying his shoe-laces.

'And to what do I owe the honour of your presence?' Raine asked with slow deliberation, almost like a drunk, finding it difficult to enunciate.

'It is my duty to inform you that I've authorised the order for your transfer to Brinstead Manor Hospital for a period of twenty-eight days for observation. My signature makes it all legal and above board.'

The West Indian nurse was now standing up. Having fixed Raine's shoe-laces, she was now knotting his tie. Raine looked at the Mental Health Officer over her shoulder.

'You signed the authorisation while I was unconscious?'

'Keep still, please, Mr Raine,' said the nurse, 'while I fix your tie.'

'I'll fix him,' said Raine.

It was not the sort of language he'd ever imagined hearing himself use, but then he'd never imagined finding himself in a situation remotely akin to this. In fact, a year ago he would not have believed that anybody, layman or lawyer, could be subjected to so outrageous a violation of personal liberty—and in a hospital, at that. He would have been most suspicious of any witness under oath who told such an improbable tale.

Raine tried to get to his feet, but found that he had not sufficiently recovered from the 'sedative' to stand unaided. He swayed and would have fallen had the nurse not put an arm round him.

'Take it easy, Mr Raine.'

His face was shiny with perspiration. He was conscious of a numbing pain as if he had been hit in the solar plexus, so that he was grateful to the nurse for easing him back on to the bed. He could not see one Mental Health Officer, but several and they were all talking at once.

'The order had already been signed by Doctors Shiplake and Maynard,' they were saying. 'So my signature was a mere formality.'

'And from what Act does your authority derive?' Raine asked.

'The Mental Health Act of 1959. As a barrister, surely you should be familiar with it? If not I'm sure they will have a copy of it at Brinstead.'

The man was being impertinent, of course. Raine asked for his name.

'Beardmore. I'll give you my card.'

'Don't bother. I'll remember it. I'll remember it.'

A chromium-plated wheelchair was pushed up the bedside by one of the porters who had so recently witnessed Raine's discomfiture, not to say humiliation. It was the Spanish youth who with the aid of the West Indian nurse proceeded to help Raine into the chair, tucking a blanket around his knees.

Staff Nurse Frimley arrived to supervise his departure, even shaking hands with him as if it were a matter for congratulation, and Mr Beardmore called out, 'Have a good time in the country, old chap.'

Then the porter trundled him out into the corridor and up the slope into the yard where a mini-bus type of ambulance was waiting. Beyond the gates Raine saw the normal world of omnibuses, mostly red but with one painted in crazy, psychedelic colours to advertise a firm of bookmakers.

The Spaniard helped him out of the wheelchair and up the steps into the ambulance. Although it was white, Raine had a feeling that he was stepping into a Black Maria. He had no time to speculate further. The ambulance door slammed. The engine revved up.

It was only then he became aware that he was to have a custodian on the journey. It was a youth with shoulder-length hair, wearing a white coat, which was quite misleading as he certainly was not a doctor and did not appear to have any insignia of nursing qualification. Raine presumed he was what is euphemistically and officially known as a nursing 'auxiliary'.

This youth said, 'Take a pew, mate.'

Raine sat down. The youth sat next to him.

'Been to the Manor before?'

'No.'

They were cruising past St James's Park. Couples were entwined on the grass and under the trees. Older people were feeding the birds. Beyond the shrubbery, Raine glimpsed the red tunics of military bandsmen and the sheen of instruments, but he heard no sound. It was as if he was already encapsulated from the world. Beyond the bandsmen's brass and pipeclay, he saw the white cone of the tea house.

Raine's custodian started whistling. Raine winced and closed his eyes, feigning sleep.

'Tired, mate?'

Raine did not reply.

2

WHEN HE OPENED his eyes he saw a yellow AA sign pointing the way to Esher. Soon they passed the weather-beaten milestone outside the Orleans Arms. They were now in stockbroker, solicitor, chartered accountant and property-developer country: detached houses, two- and three-car garages, coach lamps and brass dolphin door knockers; the trim lawns of *au pair* land, Walt Disneyish topiary and greenhouses, wattle fencing and salvaged London street lamps inside mock lych gates. Here all the pubs had wall-to-wall carpeting and new pewter tankards.

Raine could remember more than one candle-lit dinner in these parts. Here were all the outward signs of well-ordered, middle-class prosperity and sanity. There were more golf courses in this county than any other in the country—and more mental hospitals.

On the right the new Sandown Park grandstand was going up. The vast concrete structure looked more like a football stadium than a race-course. On the left was the old Bear Inn. Further along was the country club where he'd stayed so often when he'd been courting Veronica and where they had first made love.

Another mile along the Portsmouth road and the mini-bus turned into Brinstead Manor Hospital. The gravel drive had once been tree-lined. Raine wondered aloud whether elm disease might be the cause of the arboreal slaughter, the drive now being lined with raw stumps, but his custodian almost gleefully volunteered the information that a patient had but recently climbed one of the trees with a rope, which he had fastened to a branch and then hanged himself. He was found dangling at dawn.

Obviously no effort was spared in this place to protect patients from their own folly; even the trees were not spared. The contractors who had felled the trees had left a trade sign behind. It announced: TREE SURGEONS. Some wit, presumably a patient, had daubed out the word TREE and replaced it with MIND.

In the grounds was a shop where it seemed visitors could buy confectionery and soft drinks for their less fortunate friends or relatives within. It was also a sub-post office. Raine's custodian asked the driver to stop there; it was the first week of the football season and he was anxious to post his Littlewoods.

He left the ambulance door open, but the driver was looking over his shoulder, fag drooping from his mouth as he surveyed Raine. Observation. His custodian came out, chewing gum, looking more like a house painter than ever.

The original Brinstead Manor housed the administrative staff. The wards, spreading out fanwise, were army huts, *circa* 1914-18. When practising at the Bar Raine had often visited prisons to interview clients on remand awaiting trial—the bad boys who were not allowed bail. It soon became evident that the procedure of reception at Brinstead Manor Hospital was not so very different from prison routine. Except that it was, if anything, more degrading.

It was very soon made clear to him that he was not so much a patient as a prisoner. The patient was left in no doubt that he was in custody. Raine still found it difficult to believe that it really was happening to him. Come to think of it, he found it difficult to believe that it could happen to anybody in his right mind. Ah, there was the rub. Dr Emrys Shiplake had decided that he wasn't in his right mind and he, Roland John Raine, barrister at law, had no right to gainsay it.

Attempted suicide was no longer a crime. Coroners no longer pronounced verdicts to the effect that some unfortunate had killed himself while the balance of his mind was disturbed. Yet under the 1959 Act the man or woman who attempted suicide and failed could be locked up as a potential danger to himself or herself. No welfare state could be more concerned about the individual's welfare than that.

From now on he, Roland John Raine, Q.C., was not to be regarded as a fully-fledged person. He, a Queen's Counsel, was to be regarded as not fully responsible for his actions. He was not even to be permitted to wear his own clothes.

He was told to undress, then handed a pair of pyjamas that

would have been a good fit for the late Mr Laurel and a dressing gown, apparently knitted of wire wool, that would have comfortably enfolded the form of Mr Laurel's partner, Mr Hardy. The dressing gown had no cord but was fastened by one button the size of a small saucer. The aperture for this button was somewhat larger. He was handed a pair of imperfectly darned, once-white socks and a pair of down-at-heel slippers.

In this garb, which had the smell of a job-lot acquired at the closing-down sale of Buchenwald, he was escorted to the recreation room, more truthfully a hut. It was adequately, even pleasantly furnished. There were Renoir and Monet prints on the wall, armchairs, sofas, red-topped tables that might have come from a Wimpey bar and a scattering of journals, of the *Reveille, Tit-Bits* and *Weekend* level. There was also that ubiquitous panacea, a colour television set.

There were some forty men in the place and it was thick with cigarette smoke. Some of the men were sitting at the tables, playing cards or dominoes. Others watched the telly. One was solving a jigsaw puzzle. Some stood in almost conspiratorial *tête-à-tête* groups, over the shoulders glancing. Here and there were newcomers sitting alone, vacant-eyed and showing signs of withdrawal, all traumatic with shock at the very realisation of finding themselves in the place, manifestly wishing to keep themselves to themselves, anxious to demonstrate that they did not really belong here, that their presence was the result of some hideous mistake. Superficially, it could have been a working men's temperance club, if such places exist, except for one bizarre aspect. All but the white-coated nursing auxiliaries were wearing night attire as fetching as that worn by Raine. He could not help feeling that he had been shanghaied to some ludicrous all-male pyjama party.

He stood just inside the door, aware that many eyes were scrutinising the newcomer, and he was acutely self-conscious—more so than he had ever been in his life, not being prone to it. The nursing orderly who had conducted him there gave a nudge.

'Get in, mate. Make yerself at home.'

Raine replied that he had no wish to make himself at home, but was informed that this was what they all said at first and that he'd soon 'settle in'.

Then he heard his name called.

'Mr Raine!'

One of the card players had left the table and was hurrying towards him, hand outstretched. He walked rather like an orang-utan, and was grinning like a chimpanzee. His name was Oates and he was known in the underworld—inevitably—as Quaker.

Charlie 'Quaker' Oates was pumping Raine's hand until it hurt. The criminal career of Charles Oates had a unique aspect. He had a long list of convictions for breaking and entering various branches of Woolworths. Following one such depredation, it had fallen to Raine to defend him at the London Sessions.

Raine had interviewed Oates at Brixton Prison where the Woolworths' basher was on remand, awaiting trial.

Raine had asked him, 'Explain one thing to me. Why pick on Woolworths everytime? Why not Marks and Sparks, British Home Stores, Littlewoods?'

Whereupon Charlie Oates had explained that many years ago his parents had owned what was then called a general store in Lambeth. Woolworths bought the adjoining block and there opened one of their familiar red- and gold-faced emporiums. Mr and Mrs Oates Snr went out of business.

A few months later young Charlie Oates got his first sentence, Borstal, for breaking and entering the same Woolworths. Undeterred, he had been breaking and entering branches of Woolworths ever since.

Raine decided, not very hopefully, to use this as a plea of mitigation. Pleading guilty on behalf of his client, he submitted that Oates was not really a bad man. Rightly or wrongly, Oates had been motivated by the fact that many years ago his parents had been deprived of their livelihood, allegedly, by this mammoth organisation. It had become a fixation in the son's mind and the robberies he had carried out were his form of protest, deplorable though it might be. Both his parents had since died, but he was devoted to their memory and obsessed by the idea that they had suffered a grievous injustice.

It was a meretricious plea, but it succeeded. Oates was given a suspended sentence, the only act of clemency he'd ever known.

Unfortunately, 'Quaker' failed to turn over a new leaf. Once again he demonstrated his filial devotion in an unlawful manner and on this occasion there was no Raine to defend him. However, counsel pursued the same line which Raine had originated, but with not quite the same happy result.

This time the judge sent the culprit for psychiatric treatment.

'And so here I am and it's worse'n any nick I ever been in. If this is a hospital, give me the Warehouse any day. But never mind about me, Mr Raine. What about you? How come? I couldn't believe me eyes when I saw you come through that door and that monkey give you a nudge. You, of all people, in a karzy like this. How come? I don't get it.'

'Neither do I,' said Raine. 'You see, I took an overdose.'

Oates nodded sagely, full of understanding, genuinely more concerned about Raine's incarceration than his own.

'Tried to give y'self the old one-two, eh? Ah well, we all feel like that from time to time, but that's no crime. I suppose they done you on the 1959 Mental Health Act, eh?'

For an uneducated man, Charlie 'Quaker' Oates was remarkably well informed on current affairs, particularly legislation, having a vested interest as it were.

'Diabolical Act that, Mr Raine,' he observed. 'Gives the quacks more power than the bogeys. Can you imagine what a scream there'd be if a couple of bogeys could put a villain inside just by signing a bit of paper? No trial, no nothing. There'd be murders, I tell you, there'd be murders. But a couple of quacks can get innocent people put away without so much as by-your-leave nor nothing.'

Oates' voice was hoarse with indignation. No persons are more concerned about the wrongful deprivation of personal liberty than wrong-doers themselves. The most solemn oath that the professional lawbreaker can take is 'On my liberty'.

'If this is progress,' he went on, 'then give me the bad old days. Come'n take a load off your feet.'

Oates led Raine to the table where he had abandoned a card game. The other three inmates were proceeding with a 'dummy' hand. Without ceremony, Oates told them to piss off. They did so without taking any apparent offence, leaving the cards scattered on the table.

Oates moved a chair towards Raine, dusting the seat.

'Well, Mr Raine,' he said. 'It's a small world, isn't it?'

'So I am beginning to discover. We do meet in the best places, don't we?'

'Last time was Brixton, you and me over a table like this in the interview room, with a screw standing outside. Well, who'd'a thought we'd meet again like this?'

'No,' said Raine. 'Who would have thought it.'

'I ... er ... wanted you as my mouthpiece last time I went up the steps,' Oates said, diffident for once. 'But the solicitors said you weren't available.'

'That's quite right. I wasn't in circulation.'

'Couldn't make it out. Thought you'd gone abroad or something. Out of the country, like. Course, I'd heard about your trouble.'

'Oh, yes. What was that?'

Raine couldn't believe that Oates would be impudent enough to refer to Veronica and Bundock, but he was wrong. Perhaps Oates didn't realise he was being impudent.

'Your missis and that git who calls himself King of the Underworld.'

'Yes, Oates, that was a bit of a blow. I should never have taken my wife to his party.'

'You know what they say, Mr Raine, about he who sups with the Devil?'

'I do, indeed. Next time I'll take a longer fork—a roasting fork.'

Raine was trying to pass it off with a flippancy he did not feel. Yet he found it less embarrassing to talk to this thorough-paced villain about an excoriating wound in his private life than to that bland savant, Dr Emrys Shiplake.

Oates drummed his knuckles on the table.

'Roasting would be too good for that git, Mr Raine. I hope he never crosses my path, that's all.'

'Let's not discuss it.'

'No. I can quite understand y'r feelings, Mr Raine.'

Oates continued drumming on the table top. He could not let the subject rest.

'I don't know what the world's coming to. But f'r you that git would be doing twenty years right now, and how does he show his gratitude? Runs off with your missis. It's villains like that that get us all a bad name. Makes one lose one's faith in human nature.'

'I'd rather not talk about it, Oates.'

He did his best to change the topic by asking Oates whether it was customary for patients to wear night attire all the time, and whether it wasn't bad for morale.

Oates made a spitting gesture. Morale? He surely didn't think they gave a fuck about patients' morale, did he? Once upon a time they put broken glass on the tops of walls around lunatic asylums to prevent the inmates escaping. Today, not satisfied with putting patients in locked wards, the mental hospital authorities had a better wheeze.

'They take our clobber away to make it more difficult to go on the trot. Talk about maximum security nicks, this place makes 'em look like playpens—and I been in most of them.'

Sitting there, Oates reminded Raine of one of those plates illustrating Lombroso's old book on criminal types, long since out of favour among students of criminology, but still remarkable in that every picture might have been culled from the up-to-date files of Scotland Yard's Criminal Records Office.

Oates jerked a square, nail-bitten thumb in the direction of a group of nursing auxiliaries lounging by the wall, hands in key-chain pockets and talking football. Take the white coats away, put rosettes on their lapels and toilet rolls in their hands, and one could see them baying on the terraces of any Association football ground.

'Look at that shower,' he sneered. 'Call 'em nurses? There isn't a qualification among the lot of 'em. Not one of 'em would qualify as a pox doctor's clerk.'

Oates shook his head in despair at what the world was coming to, knuckles again drumming on the table.

'Come to think of it, not one of 'em would qualify as a screw,' he added. 'And I thought screws were the lowest form of human life until I came here. But one thing a screw learns is to respect the rights of the cons and he thinks twice before taking liberties. Know what I mean, Mr Raine?'

'Yes, I think I know what you mean?'

'In the nick the con has rights. In a mental hospital the patient has none, believe you me.'

'I'm beginning to realise that.'

Raine had never thought the day would come when his education would be broadened by the like of Oates, but he was to realise a lot more before he was through with custodial hospitalisation.

Oates was warming to his theme.

'I tell yer, Mr Raine, there's more humanity in the Warehouse than in this so-called hospital. Take Maidstone, f'r instance. Now that's a real soft nick. I remember once the visiting magistrates put me on bread and water there on account of a little disturbance, and the gov'ner was so upset he came down to the solitaries to eat bread and water wi' me. A real Christian, that gov'ner.'

Raine laughed for the first time in days. He said he hoped the bread wasn't Mother's Pride. Oates laughed, pleased that he had been able to jolly Raine out of his despondency.

Then a coloured auxiliary approached the table.

'The Superintendent wants to see you, man,' he said to Raine.

The man's insolent manner incensed Raine.

'My name happens to be Raine.'

'Okay, Raine. Follow me.'

'Better go,' Oates breathed. 'What he means is he follows you. These nignogs don't risk walking in front of a patient.'

The attendant was out of earshot as Oates said this. He was already unlocking the door. He stood by the open door, waiting.

As Raine walked out a number of the inmates crowded around Oates, all agog. The word had gone round. Was that really the well-known mouthpiece?

'That was yesterday,' said Oates. 'Today he's just one of us.'

3

TO WHAT EXTENT he was 'just one of them' Raine appreciated on arrival at the Superintendent's office in the main building. A white card on the door announced: Dr Lionel Chepstowe. Knock.

The attendant did so. A high-pitched voice bade them enter. Dr Chepstowe was seated at a desk beneath a window which overlooked the drive and all those stumps of slaughtered trees. Raine wondered whether it was he who had given the order for the trees to be felled because a patient had hanged himself from one of the branches.

Dr Chepstowe was rotund, and his baldness seemed to exaggerate his rotundity. His pate was shiny and his eyes a very pale blue over a snub nose. He wore a pinstripe suit over a nylon shirt and with it the tie of some minor public school. Obviously he wasn't in the same league, professionally, as Dr Shiplake. He looked rather like an inferior ship's doctor.

The Superintendent had guests. Three middle-aged ladies in Women's Institute petal hats had been taking tea with him. Their prim appearance was spoiled by the lipstick smudges on the cups and pastry crumbs on their twin-setted bosoms. Raine took them to be some sort of visiting committee. They all eyed him with bright appraisal as if he were some sort of exhibit.

'Don't go, ladies,' said Dr Chepstowe, showing a nice disregard for Raine's susceptibilities. 'I just want to ask this chap a couple of questions.'

The doctor did not bother to rise or offer Raine a seat. In fact, he did not bother to look at him.

He just said, studying the committal order, 'So you're Raine.'

Raine considered that it would be superfluous to reply, although he felt tempted to retort, 'So you're Chepstowe.' No High Court judge would have been so discourteous. He felt a prison governor would have shown more civility to an old lag.

Chepstowe's next observation was even less civil.

'And you're of no fixed abode?'

Raine's professional life and training had not conditioned him to take this kind of gibe meekly. He was not meek by nature and too many years in what Dr Shiplake had chosen to refer to as 'the cut and thrust' of the criminal courts had not rendered him amenable to plain rudeness.

'I would say that as from here and now I am of a very fixed abode and it is not one I would care to recommend to an under-privileged leper.'

Raine was pleased to see that his retort had got under the Superintendent's shrimp-hued skin. The doctor's voice became even more high-pitched.

'Don't deliberately misinterpret me. Where do you live? Where was your last fixed address?'

'If you are really interested,' said Raine. 'I am listed in *Who's Who.*'

Chepstowe was convinced that Raine was again being offensive, implying that *he* would never be in *Who's Who.*

'This is not a public library,' he said.

'You surprise me. However, if you really wish to know my last fixed address I am also listed in the telephone directory.

'Excuse me, ladies.'

Dr Chepstowe apologised to his guests as he reached for the L to R section of the London directory, managing to give that sort of raised eyebrows glance intended to indicate that here was an example of the tiresomeness and mulish aggression of some of the patients under his wing.

The ladies were both embarrassed and fascinated, all their sympathy being for the doctor, poor man. One sipped at an empty tea-cup, eyes directed at Raine over the rim. Another dusted pastry crumbs from her bosom. The third caressed her lips with a tissue, surveying herself in a flapjack mirror.

The Superintendent eventually located the entry.

'There are two addresses here,' he said, almost accusingly.

'The one at Hare Court, Inner Temple, was my address in

chambers,' Raine explained. 'It is no longer valid as I am no longer in chambers.'

'Then it's the Dulwich address?'

'That was my last residential address, yes.'

'Then you're in the wrong hospital,' Dr Chepstowe snapped.

'Thanks for the good news. When can I leave?'

'You cannot. You have to be transferred to Epsom, to Horseley West Hospital. You're in the wrong catchment area. Mental health patients living south of the Thames go to Horseley West. Patients living north of the Thames come here.'

'Then you're detaining me improperly.'

'You have been quite properly detained under Section 25 of the Mental Health Act. You have only yourself to blame for having been sent here. If you had co-operated with the staff at West End Central and given your address in the first place you would have been sent to the appropriate hospital. Now you'll have to stay here until I can arrange transport.'

He turned in his swivel chair to replace the directory.

'That will be all.'

The nursing auxiliary touched Raine on the arm, then plucked at the sleeve of the wire-wool dressing gown. Raine, however, had no intention of being dismissed in such a cavalier and condescending fashion.

'You'll pardon me,' he said. 'That is not all. I have been brought here against my will. I have been technically assaulted—by being forced to take a heavily sedative drug—and I wish to challenge the authority of the order committing me here.'

'You can only do that before a High Court judge.'

This was the supreme irony. He, Roland J. Raine, being told the Law by the Superintendent of a mental hospital.

'And what machinery exists here for approaching a High Court judge? May I use your telephone?'

'No, you may not. You must first make application to the Courts in writing.'

'Then perhaps you can give me a sheet of writing paper and an envelope?'

'Stationery can be bought at the hospital shop.'

'I have no money.'

'Then I suggest that you wait until you get to Horseley West before you start agitating.'

'I am not agitating. I merely wish my liberty to be restored.'

'Liberty to polish yourself off?' It was a sneer.

'That is my concern and mine only.'

'Not entirely. I might also tell you that no High Court judge can agree to your discharge from custodial hospitalisation unless your next of kin assumes responsibility for you.'

Raine could have laughed. He could have laughed his head off. He could have fallen over. He felt at that moment as if he really was about to take leave of his senses.

The idea of Veronica, the ever-loving wife who had left him for a notorious gangster, standing up in Court and saying that she would be responsible for him was too excruciating. He wondered what learned law officers of the Crown could frame such asinine Acts. More, he wondered what sort of legislators could put them on the Statute Book.

Raine paused at the door. He looked at Chepstowe. He looked at the petal-hatted ladies.

'This really is a sanctuary for bruised souls,' he said.

Then, with a slight bow to the ladies, he walked out, followed by his escort.

Distantly a bell rang. Like a school bell. No, a prison bell.

'That's the supper bell. Turn left for the dining recess.'

'Rather early for supper, isn't it?'

'I said turn left, man.'

'I have no wish to eat.'

'Turn left for the dining recess, man.'

Raine shrugged and turned left, listening to the flip-flop of his down-at-heel slippers along the corridor. Access to the dining recess, or hut, was through a sleeve like those to be found at airports.

The ludicrously-attired patients were shuffling into a queue before a self-service counter, manned by patients, similarly attired except for white aprons buttoned—not tied—over the dressing gowns.

Not proposing to join the queue, Raine sat down at an unoccupied table and looked around. Here too there were prints on the walls, mostly from Constable: The Haywain, Willy Lot's Cottage, Salisbury Cathedral. All very restful.

Oates beckoned to him from the front of the queue.

'Better come and get some of this swill, Mr Raine.'

Raine shook his head, but could not help admiring the man's effrontery in giving public utterance to his opinion of the hospital food. It was as if he was trying to provoke the attendants, but as the food was prepared by the patients for the patients, they were indifferent. It was policy to let the pigs grunt.

Raine thought wryly of Benchers' dinners, and of all that tawny port circulating. He thought, too, of dinner parties at his own home, with judges and cabinet ministers and wives as guests, their chauffeurs eating in the kitchen and flirting with the *au pairs*.

And now this.

In another ten years he, too, might have become a judge, perhaps not always a sober judge—though that would have been no drawback. He'd known one judge who always had Gordon's gin in the water flagon on the bench, and another who had vodka.

Oates came to the table with two suppers on the tray.

'Best to eat,' he said. 'Don't give those pox doctors' clerks an excuse for forcible feeding.'

'Are you allowed to take two portions?'

'No, but them slags on the serving hatch do as I tell 'em.'

Oates pushed a cardboard plate in front of Raine and with it some eating utensils made of material similar to that used for the spoons that come with ice-cream tubs.

He watched Oates taste the yellowish splurge on the plate, vividly decorated with tomato sauce.

'What is it?'

'I think it's tapioca mixed with the left-overs of this morning's porridge,' said Oates. 'Anyway, better eat—or those ponces'll be sticking a tube down y'r gullet.'

Raine suddenly thought of Strasbourg geese being force-fed by old peasant women, who held them fast between their black-skirted knees. Well, he didn't anticipate eating *foie gras* in the near future.

Oates again pointed at Raine's untouched plate.

'Best eat, Mr Raine,' he urged.

'If I could scrape the food off I might be tempted to eat the plate.'

Oates roared with a laughter that Raine thought the remark scarcely merited. So loud was his laughter that the white-coated attendants looked across, wondering what anybody could find to laugh at in this place. Only the real nut-cases laughed like that.

'Tell me, Mr Raine, what happened in the office with that—excuse the language—prick Chepstowe?'

'I'd like to circumcise him without benefit of anaesthetic,' said Raine. 'And with a blunt scalpel.'

Again Oates roared with manic laughter.

'Glad to see you've kept y'r sense of humour, Mr Raine. That's good, that is. Know the old saying? He who laughs last.'

Raine nodded. Oates was a great one for old sayings. In fact, if he had not know so much about Oates he might have been tempted to believe that he was just a good-natured simpleton whose life was ruled by home-spun philosophy, a harmless fellow whose innate goodness was belied by his unfortunate appearance.

The terrible thing was that Raine was grateful for the man's company. Hospitalisation was the great leveller, not death. In an odd way their positions had been reversed. Oates was now *his* adviser. It was preposterous.

'It seems I am in the wrong hotel,' Raine told him.

'How come?'

'This salubrious establishment apparently is for the benefit of those who live north of the Thames. I'm in the wrong catchment area, and I must admit I do feel a bit like a fish out of water.'

'Where they sending you then?'

'Epsom.'

'Which one? There's fifteen mental hospitals around Epsom.'

'Horseley West, I think he said.'

'Jeeze, that's a real nut house.'

'How do you know?'

'For one thing, Mitchell the Axe was there. Then there was Toby the Tool and Frank the Flasher. They don't come any nuttier than them three.'

'And now there's going to be Raine the Bar.'

Once more Oates roared with a laughter as mindless as that produced by a television studio audience.

'You'll find Horseley West and this place as different as chalk and cheese,' he said when his merriment had subsided.

'In what way?'

'Well, as I say, there's real nut cases there. There's no real nut cases here. Most of them are just as sane as you and me.'

Raine, not knowing quite what to say to this parenthesis of personalities, kept quiet.

'They're all malingerers here who ought to be doing bird—and believe you me, Mr Raine, that's what they'd prefer to be doing.'

'I almost think I'd prefer to be doing it myself,' said Raine.

'How does the day go here?' he added.

'In the mornings there's all the skivvy work to do, the washing and scrubbing, sweeping and polishing floors, just like in the nick, except in the nick you get a few bob's wages at the end of the week. Here you get nothing, not a light. We're not so much patients as an unpaid labour force. I tell you, Mr Raine, it's scandalous.'

'And in the afternoons?'

'There's what they call Occupational Therapy.'

'Consisting of what?'

'Oh, some young bint comes along and teaches us to make soft toys or baskets. Me, I'd sooner sew mailbags.'

'And what about the so-called psychiatric treatment?'

'After the first time, I told 'em to stuff it. It was a lady shrinker. Know what she asked me? Had I ever, as a boy, seen my mother and old man on the job together? I told her I thought she was being downright disgusting.

'Of course, that was a black mark against me. I wasn't co-operating. When you don't co-operate you're considered mental, see? It's only when you does co-operate that they say you're responding to treatment. Nice, isn't it?

'Then if you still don't co-operate you get electric shock treatment two or three times a week. That's why most of the fifteen hundred patients here are like walking zombies.'

'Fifteen hundred!'

'Eight hundred women and seven hundred men. There's always more skirt in nut houses than trousers. Don't ask me why, Mr Raine.'

'I won't, but I can tell you what Daniel Defoe wrote about women in mad houses nearly three hundred years ago. Ever heard of Daniel Defoe?'

'Sure, he wrote *Robinson Crusoe*, didn't he?'

'Well, yes, but he was also the first journalist. He campaigned against what he called the "vile practice much in vogue among what are called the better sort, but are in reality the worst sort, of putting their wives in Mad Houses at every Whim or Dislike, that they may be more secure and undisturbed in their Debaucheries". He said it was "the height of Barbarity and Injustice in a Christian country". He said it was "a clandestine Inquisition, nay worse. How many Ladies and Gentlewomen are hurried away to these houses, which ought to be suppressed or at least subjected to daily Examination?" '

'Did old Robinson Crusoe say that? Pity he's not alive today. He'd be working on the *Sun*. Things haven't changed much, Mr Raine, have they? There was a case only a couple of year ago of two unmarried mothers who'd been kept in a mental hospital for fifty years apiece all on account of having had illegitimate kids. It's enough to make you shiver, isn't it?'

'Oates, I am shivering.'

'You know something, Mr Raine, I'm sorry you're leaving here in one way. You'd be great in the Discussion Groups.'

'What do you talk about?'

'Ourselves.'

'That must be fun.'

'Not as much fun as the dances.'

'Quite frankly, Oates, I can't quite imagine you as an exponent of the light fantastic.'

'Oh, they put me on the door.'

Oates went on to explain that not all patients were invited to the Saturday night dances. It was a highly coveted privilege.

'Excuse me,' he said, taking a cigarette butt from behind his ear and lumbering across to one of the auxiliaries for a light.

The white-coated attendant ignored Oates's request for several minutes whilst he continued chatting to his colleagues. When he did give Oates a light it was from the end of his own cigarette.

A big, lubbery-looking fellow with Mongoloid features came up to Raine's table, stabbed a finger in the direction of the untouched supper and then pointed at his own mouth.

Raine nodded. The feeble-minded, deaf mute grabbed the plate and hurried away.

'That's another thing,' Oates said when he came back, smoke peeling out of his hirsute nostrils, 'We have to go to those toe-rags every time we want a light.'

'In that case,' said Raine, 'I'm glad I don't smoke.'

He went on to ask Oates about the dances. Were they, in fact, pyjama dances? No, said the Quaker, for such social events the patients were allowed to wear their own clothes. The music was execrable, more often than not being provided by the patients themselves, but generally speaking a good time was had by all.

'It's a great night for shagging,' said Oates. 'The shop sells French letters but a lot of the women would sooner you didn't wear one, on account of their wanting to get a bun in the oven—so they can get out of here.'

'And the administration turns a blind eye to all this?'

'A blind eye! I'd say they encourage it. They reckon it releases pent-up tensions.'

'No doubt,' said Raine. 'And probably causes a few too.'

'Mind you, they're all at it—them toe-rags as well.'

He nodded in the direction of the white-coated custodians.

'And where does this activity take place?'

'Oh, all over, all over.'

Oates made sweeping gestures.

'In the grounds, in doorways, in the bushes. A right proper old orgy.'

'The patients have access to the grounds?'

'On dance nights, yes. It's held in the ball room in the old house, y'see.'

'Nobody runs away?'

'They're too busy *yentzing* to think about going on the trot. Oh, it's a rare old sight. Then again, everybody is dressed in their own clothes except they has to wear slippers.'

'A sort of soft-shoe shuffle?'

'Sort of.'

Raine glanced around. It was quite obvious that many of the inmates were just feeble-minded. Some were picking up the sticky food with their fingers and cramming it into their mouths. Others were licking their plates. One man's nose dripped mucous into his supper. He ate with relish.

They went back to the recreation room where card-playing and television-watching was resumed, as well as games of draughts, snakes and ladders, ludo—and one chess contest. There were *kibitzers* around the chess players. Raine got up and joined them.

Within a few minutes he came back to the table where Oates was still seated looking very glum, chin in hands.

'You said everybody here is as sane as you and I,' said Raine. 'That pair aren't playing chess at all. They're moving the pieces to no known rules.'

'Mr Raine, in this place they make up their own rules. Why abide by the outside rules?'

Then one of the chess players upset the board, jumped on to his chair and addressed everybody. Everybody, because it was impossible not to hear him. He had the voice of a fairground barker.

'The Lord looketh down from heaven! And what does He see? Us lot here! Yes, from His place of habitation He looketh down upon us. May He who establishes peace in His high heaven grant peace of mind to us down here below. The Lord shall guard thy going out and thy coming in!'

At this a cheer went up, accompanied by much laughter and derisive whistling. There was also some ineffective stamping of slippered feet.

Some yelled for more from this instant preacher. Apparently he was an amusing turn when the mood took him, but tonight he seemed to have no staying power and got down to retrieve the scattered chessmen, crawling about the floor on hands and knees and barking like a Pekinese. Facially he resembled one.

This man who had just been calling upon the Lord was now scrabbling around Raine's feet.

'Do you mind, sir? Your fucking foot's on my Queen.'

Raine lifted one foot, then the other. There was nothing beneath either of them except the floor, but the man on all fours made a gesture of scooping up chess pieces.

A bell rang. The fun and games were over. It was bedtime and, like a crowd of overgrown children being sent up early for naughtiness, they shuffled and flip-flapped in their slippers towards the ward, queueing up *en route* at the inadequate lavatories, whose cubicles were doorless. A patient had once drowned himself in a lavatory pan, having first blocked it up to stop the water running away. So they took all the doors off.

A man hangs himself from the branch of a tree. So all the trees are slaughtered.

'One night,' said Oates, 'somebody will suffocate himself with a pillow. Then we'll have no pillows.'

What was the logic behind such daft decisions? Again, Raine asked aloud what sort of sanctuary for bruised souls this was, and what sort of people were responsible for running it and what were their qualifications for acting as custodians for the allegedly mentally disturbed?

What sort of healing process was this? Why this needless shame and degradation? What sanity was there in putting Impressionist prints on the walls and cutting down all the trees? Who were the sane?

Raine felt like paraphrasing Falstaff: What is sanity? A word.... Who hath it? He that died o' Wednesday?

He had nearly died o' Wednesday himself, but had been frustrated in the attempt, brought back to life into a strange world even more disagreeable than that which he had attempted to leave.

Perhaps it would have been more apposite to quote Hamlet: 'Why, look you now, how unworthy a thing you make of me!'

In this present predicament Raine was glad that, many years ago, he had read Literature as well as Law. The latter provided cold comfort and he could echo Montaigne's aphorism that the very Laws of Justice cannot subsist without some commixture of Injustice.

'Know thyself,' was written in the Temple of Delphi. Roland John Raine had for the greater part of his adult life been convinced that he knew himself. Every morning when he shaved he had quoted Claude Le Petit: *Le monde est plein de fous, et qui n'en veut pas voir Doit se tenir tout seul, et casser son miroir.* The world was full of fools, and he who would not see it should live alone and smash his mirror.

Now he realised that he had not known himself as well as he had imagined. Three years ago he could not have imagined a life situation so unhappy that he would be induced to attempt to end that life. He was not as resilient as he had thought.

With these thoughts, Raine eventually slept. When he awakened he saw Oates pushing the early morning tea trolley. He got the impression that Oates was a sort of 'trusty'. Little they know, Raine thought; but Oates, having spent so many years in various kinds of custody, knew that custodians were by the very nature of their job unfitted for anything else and lazy withal. So he who made himself indispensable made his own incarceration so much the more bearable.

'How many sugars, Mr Raine?'

'None, thanks.'

Oates leaned closer towards him.

'Sure you don't want no sugar, Mr Raine?' he said in a voice that was just a little too loud.

Then he added in what was no more than a whisper, 'Can I do anything for you on the outside?'

'Why? Are you being discharged?'

Oates shook his head. He continued to whisper while pretending to dole out spoonfuls of sugar.

'No, but I've decided to have it away. I'm going on the trot. I can't take no more of this. The way I see it they won't wear me refusing to take their psychiatric treatment and I'll be sent back to the Old Bailey for sentence. Well, before that happens I've got a lot of unfinished business on the outside, including a call on that git Bundock.'

Raine replied in a whisper.

'For God's sake, Oates, forget that. It's none of your business.'

'No?' said Oates. 'Then I'm going to make it my business. Nobody takes liberties with friends of mine and I regard you as a friend of mine, Mr Raine, if you'll excuse the familiarity.'

'Oates, you cannot take the law into your own hands.'

'No? It strikes me everybody else does. Sure you don't want no messages delivered on the outside?'

'Oates, promise me one thing.'

'Anything within reason.'

'Leave Bundock alone.'

'I'm sorry, Mr Raine, but that's not within reason.'

Then he continued pushing the tea trolley, calling out, 'How many sugars?'

4

RAINE WAS NOT unversed in the art of persuasion, but he realised that nothing he could say would convince Oates that it was not his duty to inflict some grievous harm upon the person of Harry George Bundock.

Long before psychiatry became fashionable there was a saying popular among the unlearned to the effect that one might as well talk to a block of wood as argue with some people. Charlie 'Quaker' Oates was one such person. If Freud, Jung and Adler had all risen from their respective graves, and each devoted a month of psychiatric Sundays to analysing him, they could not have talked even the hind leg off his donkey mind.

In any case Raine had no further opportunity of talking to Oates. After breakfast of tinned tomatoes on fried bread, the Quaker went off with the brooms and buckets squad because these chores gave him opportunities for perambulation and access to the grounds.

Later in the day a 'nursing' auxiliary brought Raine's clothes in a pillow-case, telling him to change in one of the 'side wards' as the dormitory wards were off limits after breakfast. The 'side wards' were actually padded cells without any furniture whatsoever, their floors sloping and with gullies running down to a drain.

The young man who had accompanied Raine to the 'side ward', sometimes known as the seclusion ward, looked as if he had just graduated from the ranks of skinheads. Thin, pale-faced, crop-headed, trousers hitched too high over ankles, built-up, buckled shoes with square toes.

'Git y'r clobber on.'

As Raine extracted the garments from the pillow-slip he realised that they were wet as well as crumpled. And they exuded a most unpleasant smell.

He looked at the white-coated, crop-headed youth in disgust mingled with disbelief, wondering what Comprehensive school, what State-aided family background had spawned this creature.

'Somethin' wrong?'

'Yes, somebody has urinated on my clothes.'

The youth took a deep drag on his cigarette.

'Well, you was the last to wear 'em, weren't you?'

'They have been urinated on—not in. And quite recently, I would say.'

The youth tried to blow a smoke ring at him.

'So you'd say that, would you? You reckon you're an expert on piss, do you?'

Raine was in his forties; this obscene youth was in his twenties, and looked just as vicious as he was disgusting. But it was not this that deterred Raine from resorting to physical action. The years of alcoholism in which he had indulged since Veronica's departure had not entirely impaired his physique. As young Dr Maynard had said, all things considered, he was in pretty good shape. At Cambridge he had acquired a double Blue, one for boxing. In more recent years he had ridden in—and won—Bar point-to-points. Sorely tempted as he was to clout the filthy tormentor in a white coat, Raine stayed his hand.

Twenty years at the Bar had taught him to beware both precipitate words and actions; and that the greater the provocation the greater the need to count—mentally—up to a hundred and ten. It was an axiom of the Bar that to lose your temper was to lose your case.

It could only have been by design that he had been told to dress in this padded cell. Moreover, he was quite sure that this crop-headed custodian had colleagues in the vicinity.

And so it proved. Another orderly arrived and with him the ambulance driver. The new orderly was unhealthily overweight. If the first one was a graduate from the ignoble fraternity of skin-heads this one was a Hell's Angel gone to seed.

'What's going on 'ere?' he demanded. 'We been waiting twenty minutes.'

Raine ignored him, folded his arms and asked the crop-headed youth his name.

'Can't yer read?'

The identity tag over the pocket of the youth's white coat revealed him to be a Nigel Fox.

'Why ain't he dressed?' asked the newcomer, who was to be Raine's custodian on the trip to Horseley West. Nigel Fox tried to burlesque Raine's accent.

'The gentleman says he can't dress because somebody's urinated on his clothes. Who'd ever do such a thing I can't imagine.'

'Look, matey,' said the overweight auxiliary. 'You got a choice. You ivor wear y'r own gear—pissed on or not—or you wears restrictive clothing, see?'

Restrictive clothing. Euphemisms out of the mouths of louts. Restrictive clothing indeed. A strait jacket.

Raine looked at the three youngsters, all of them eager for a spot of patient bashing. On the outside they would probably have gone in for Pakistani bashing or queer bashing. Or Mugging. The National Health Service really had to scrape the barrel.

Roland John Raine, Q.C. began to dress.

As the mini-bus ambulance approached Horseley West Hospital he could see the Epsom Grandstand towering above the Downs and a horse-box winding its way up to the Durdans. Raine felt envious of the horse.

The horse would be well-groomed. His coat would shine like a conker. His tail would be a proud plume which he would switch if annoyed. His eye would have a gleam. His lad, an assiduous valet, would be devoted.

Whereas he, Roland John Raine, sometime barrister at law, felt like a reeking scarecrow on which foxes lifted their legs. He kept these thoughts to himself, wondering how the house psychiatrist would interpret them. He could imagine the first entry on one of those scrupulously kept medical cards from which case histories are built: on arrival patient R.J.R. compared himself unfavourably with a horse, believing himself to be a scarecrow.'

('Smythe, how would you analyse this patient?'

'It's quite obvious, sir. He is suffering from manic depressive psychosis caused by the excessive manifestation of his *mortido* over his *libido*. He is a victim of hallucinations and persecution neuroses.'

'An example, Smythe?'
'Yes sir. He imagines that the nurses foul his clothing.')

Raine was not so prejudiced as to discount all psychiatric dogma, but neither did he subscribe to it in its complex entirety. It was by no means an exact science, much of it being based upon surmise and theory. A knowledge of Czerny's 101 does not in itself make a concert pianist—and the mind of man was surely infinitely more intricate and hypersensitive than a keyboard.

So he had no intention of allowing any mental piano tuners to go to work on him, no intention of allowing second year students to play Freudian scales up and down *his* mind. He was not going to submit to hour-long confessionals so that his interrogators could then presume to know more about Roland John Raine than he did himself.

His life had been saved at the West End Central Hospital, but the indignity of the stomach pump was less than that which was now being inflicted on him in the name of custodial care. He had ceased to be regarded as a socially responsible person. His self-esteem was to be assassinated in the name of medical science. From now he was to be card-indexed, re-assessed, reduced in social status, not permitted to make decisions for himself and to be at all times at the mercy of louts in white coats masquerading as nurses. This was not hospitalisation. It was degradation. No wonder Erving Goffman had written that psychiatric hospitalisation was more destructive of self than criminal incarceration.

Raine found that Oates had not exaggerated when he described Horseley West as 'a real nut house'. At Brinstead Manor the general atmosphere had been one of apathy. Entering the recreation room at Horseley was like going backstage at a three-ring circus, with every performer rehearsing his own thing.

One inmate had tied himself into Yoga-like knots and was viewing Raine from an upside-down line of vision, head between his knees and backside in the air. An old man was playing hop-scotch, and a Malay a violin—in the excruciating way that only Orientals can play the fiddle. Even this noise was not quite so unnerving as that produced by a large man who kept putting his fingers between his teeth and emitting a shrill whistle, then yelling 'Taxi!' A young negro was ambling up and down, droning rather than singing 'Black man and white man happy together', slapping newcomers on the shoulder and shouting, 'Welcome to the club, man.' Another old man, with a gnome-like face and cauliflower ears, was shadow boxing, dressing gown flapping around his spindly legs. A youth with long blond hair was staggering to and fro, from one end of the room to the other and back again, the blurred look in his eyes indicating that he was coming out of some drug-induced 'trip'. Others, quite oblivious, read magazines or held what appeared to be discussion groups.

One feature redeemed Horseley West. The male nurses were qualified. They were a different breed entirely from the louts of Brinstead Manor and Raine could not help wondering how it came about that two establishments under the same authority could be so dissimilar in the quality of staff.

The male nurses here wore their badges or epaulettes of rank on white, short-sleeved coats that buttoned up around the neck like barbers' smocks. They were mostly in their twenties, and were well-spoken, cheerful and smiling, courteous and clean. There were no cigarettes behind ears or dirt beneath finger-nails.

They appeared to be concerned for the comfort of their patients, and the charge nurse who received Raine actually found pyjamas and dressing gown that were a reasonable fit, slippers that were down-at-heel. This one actually introduced himself.

'My name's Shawe—with an e. I'll show you the ropes. First, do you mind putting these on, Mr Raine?'

'Mind!' Raine echoed. 'I'm only too glad to get this foul-smelling suit off.'

He explained what had happened. Charge Nurse Shawe listened with apparent sympathy but was quite non-committal, and Raine realised that even this intelligent and well-disposed young man did not believe him.

It was obvious that these young men were trained to take patients' stories with a grain of psychiatric salt, particularly the stories they told on arrival which were often invented to boost their own diminished personality status, to induce sympathy or establish the fact that they were not as the other patients.

'We will have the suit sent to the cleaners, Mr Raine.'

He spoke as if it was an everyday occurrence, picking the clothes up by the tips of his fingers and dropping them into a plastic bag. A thought struck Raine.

'I say!' he said. 'You don't think I'm incontinent, do you?'

'Of course not, Mr Raine.'

It was with dismay that Raine realised that the reply carried no tone of conviction. It was with even greater dismay that he realised his very question of implied protest might have led Charge Nurse Shawe to believe just that.

'This way, Mr Raine.'

And so they went into the recreation ward where Shawe introduced him to a colleague.

'Oh, Bill. This is Mr Raine. Mr Raine, my colleague Bill Winton.'

'Pleased to meet you, Mr Raine. You probably find all this a bit strange?'

Surveying the manifold antics of the other inmates, the shadow-boxing and tumbling, shuddering to the sound of a screeching violin, piercing whistles and shouts of 'Taxi!', Raine could not even reply, unable to believe that this was not a nightmare.

'If I can give you a tip,' said Bill Winton. 'Try to avoid staring at any one individual for any length of time. Some of these chaps are apt to take offence if they imagine that you are ridiculing them.'

'It is very difficult not to stare. Where does one turn one's eyes?'

'You can always look out of the window, Mr Raine.'

'And imagine I'm at the Derby?'

Bill Winton smiled.

'That won't be for another eight months or so, will it? And by that time you'll be out of here.'

'I should hope so.'

'By the way, if you'd like to meet any of the other chaps, let me know.'

'Good God, no thank you.'

'As you wish. Well, you'll find some magazines on the table over there.'

'Thanks,' said Raine.

He sat in a green basket-work chair and looked out of the window. There was Epsom Grandstand mocking him.

Suddenly, he heard Veronica's voice.

'Sea Bird! Sea Bird! Come on, Sea Bird!'

She threw her race-card and handbag in the air, threw her arms round him, crying 'Darling, he's won, he's won!'

That was the Derby of ten years ago. A mere ten years. And now this. A vast despair seized him.

He stood up and shouted, 'For Christ's sake! Why didn't they let me die?'

None of the other inmates paid any attention to him. The shadow-boxer went on shadow-boxing. The long distance runner continued long distance running round and round the room, slippers under his arm. The Malay went on scraping his violin, the drug addict continued to fall all over the place.

Raine resumed his seat.

'Now, I really am mad,' he said to himself. 'They have succeeded in processing me into insanity.'

'It's not as bad as that.'

A benign man with a sibilant voice had taken the chair alongside him, leaning close as if to reassure and comfort. He had a cultured air.

'You're new here, aren't you?'

Raine nodded.

'You are not mad. You are merely suffering from a behaviour disorder. Your Ego is temporarily unable to keep the Id under control so that you are behaving neurotically, the Ego capitulating to the Id, thus giving vent to overt forms of behaviour which are called psychoses. Now the first step in curing a psychosis is to understand it. I will tell you how to understand it....'

'You will do nothing of the kind, Mr Bettway. Please go back to your magazine and leave Mr Raine alone.'

The speaker was the nurse, Bill Winton. It was only then that Raine realised that the man who had sat down alongside him, speaking with such sibilant concern and sympathy, was like himself wearing pyjamas and dressing gown. Like himself, he was a patient. Mr Bettway got up and, with a slightly aggrieved look, went away.

'You musn't mind Mr Bettway,' said Bill Winton. 'He's been in so many hospitals like this he imagines he's a psychiatrist.'

'He certainly knows all the jargon. Put a white coat on him and who'd know the difference?'

'I think I would,' said Bill Winton. 'What I really came over to tell you was that Dr Glazer would like to see you.'

As they left the room Mr Bettway could be heard complaining that it was a nice state of affairs when one was not allowed to help a fellow patient.

Dr Eric Glazer had a slight accent combined with a charm and very English good looks that suggested, oddly, Hungarian origins. His silver hair matched his light grey suit. He rose from his chair to greet Raine, extending his hand.

'Do sit down, Mr Raine.'

He pushed a box of cigarettes towards Raine and seemed to approve when the offer was declined. He explained that he did not smoke himself but did realise that some people unfortunately could not relax without a cigarette. This man was civilised, unlike the boorish Superintendent at Brinstead.

'You are probably finding it all rather irksome here, Mr Raine?'

'Irksome is a good word, Doctor.'

It had occurred to Raine that it might be better to co-operate after all. If he played along with them there was a reasonable chance that he might be released at the expiry of the twenty-eight days.

'But you don't think it goes far enough?'

Dr Glazer was smiling. So far, so good. He was awaiting a reply. He wanted Raine's opinion.

'I don't think any one word could be adequately descriptive,' said Raine. 'But to the newcomer it is rather, well—bewildering. When I first stepped into the recreation room I got the impression of being backstage at a circus rather than in a hospital.'

'That isn't a bad simile, Mr Raine, but I'm afraid it's a rather sad circus where all the performers are mentally sick.'

'May I ask you a question, Dr Glazer?'

'Please do.'

'Do you think I am mentally sick?'

'You are probably acutely depressed and that is a form of mental sickness.'

'If that is so, Dr Glazer, surely it would be equally true to say that exuberant spirits, *joie de vivre* if you like, is also a form of mental sickness.'

The doctor laughed.

'I can see that we are going to have some interesting discussions, Mr Raine.'

He then glanced down at a white card and sheet of buff foolscap in front of him. There, Raine thought, is my dossier. My life has been saved but my identity as I knew it and understand it is now in process of reconstruction by my medical custodians, some good, some bad, some indifferent. I am not what I think I am, but what *they* decide I am.

'In the meantime,' said Dr Glazer, 'I'd like to put you on a course of massive vitamin injections. Lack of food over a considerable period, plus a large intake of alcohol, destroys the essential vitamins. We've got to put them back. Agreed?'

Again there was a gold-capped smile. Raine agreed, but hoped there would be no mind-bending drugs. Dr Glazer assured him there would not. Sometimes they achieved more harm than good.

Raine did not say so, but he was of the opinion that his mind was already bending. He had started talking to himself. In the recreation room only a quarter of an hour ago he had yelled, at the top of his voice, for Christ's sake why didn't they let him die. It was out of character. It was not the Raine he knew.

From here, looking over Dr Glazer's head, he could see another angle of Epsom Grandstand. It badly needed a coat of paint. Some of the white woodwork was stained yellow, and it wasn't the effect of autumn sunshine.

Again he could hear Veronica's voice.

'Sea Bird! Sea Bird! Sea Bird! Come on, Sea Bird!'

He could see her now in that caramel suit of silk shantung which matched her shoulder-length hair, shimmering in the diffused sunlight in that private box, the opal brooch on her lapel matching her eyes and even her shoes. Now she was flinging her arms round him so madly and ecstatically that they might have been in a bedroom instead of on a race-course.

They went to the Derby the following year, and again she backed the winner, Charlottown. That year she was wearing a billowing tangerine dress with piqué collar and cuffs. He could hear her heels drumming on the wooden planking of the box.

'Come on, Scobie! Come on, Scobie!'

Then she had turned to him with an agonised expression on her lovely face as he lowered his binoculars.

'He *has* won, darling, hasn't he? Don't tell me it was Pretendre.'

'No, Charlottown by half a length I'd say.'

Again she'd flung her arms around him, kissing him as passionately as if they were all alone on Epsom Downs instead of in the jam-packed Grandstand.

Nine years ago. And now this.

'You seem miles away, Mr Raine.'

'As a matter of fact, Doctor, I was up in those stands, nine, ten years ago.'

'You are a racing man, Mr Raine?'

It could have been a polite conversation between two strangers in a gentlemen's club.

'It was one of my recreations.'

'And the others?'

'The theatre, music, art.'

All these pleasures Veronica had shared with him, ecstatically, almost with abandon. Then, three years ago, she had left him for a man with positively no culture, no sensitivity, no presence, no charm, not even the elements of education. A criminal. A base, evil man. Why? Surely the one person who *should* be psychoanalysed was Veronica herself? Not he, Raine.

And what answer would these omniscient psychiatrists come up with, assuming that they analysed Veronica according to their textbook theories? Not the hoary old one that at heart every woman wants to be defiled?

Dr Glazer stood up.

'It's been pleasant talking to you, Mr Raine. I'll enjoy our future discussions. We seem to have similar interests. Alas, I almost never have an opportunity to visit the theatre or hear a concert these days. Shall we say the same time tomorrow?'

Raine was looking at Dr Glazer's hat which was on top of a filing cabinet. It was a velour with a feather in the band. He felt that the doctor was just a bit vain. However.

'Thank you, Doctor. You are most kind.'

Dr Glazer opened the door for them.

'Until tomorrow then.'

Another patient was waiting outside with a male nurse in attendance. It was the punch-drunk old shadow boxer, still skipping about on his spindly legs, breathing hard and sucking on an imaginary gum-shield.

Ducking and diving, sniffing and snorting, he skipped into the Doctor's office as if it were just another gymnasium. In a way it was.

'Well,' said Bill Winton. 'That wasn't much of an ordeal, was it?'

They were walking back towards the recreation room. Unlike at Brinstead Manor, the nurse walked alongside.

'I like Dr Glazer.'

'Everybody here does.'

'I get the impression that he works hard at getting people to like him,' said Raine.

'I don't think so. With him, it's effortless. Did you notice the way old Grimble's eyes lit up when he saw him?'

'Grimble?'

'The old-time scrapper.'

'Oh, yes. How long has he been here?'

'Grimble or Dr Glazer?'

'Grimble.'

'Three years.'

'God Almighty!'

'Actually he likes it here. He was in an old people's home, but they turfed him out. The other old folk wouldn't put up with his capering around.'

'What's his trouble?'

'Basically, tertiary syphilis. But I'm talking too much. I should not discuss patients with patients.'

'I'm sorry. I shouldn't have asked you.'

'Oh, that's all right. Well, here we are.'

The key turned and he was back in the recreation room. He tried to avert his eyes from the various antics of the performers in this sad circus and studied the prints on the wall, mostly Gainsboroughs here.

Raine wondered what sort of person had the task of providing prints to adorn the walls of mental hospitals. Who chose the French Impressionists for Brinstead Manor and portraits for West Horseley? He picked up a copy of *Weekend*. Who chose the reading material?

'My dear chap!'

The speaker was a man of about his own age, and somehow he managed to look almost dandyish even in wire-wool dressing gown and chain-gang striped pyjamas. There was even a crease to the pyjama legs and his slippers looked as if they had been Cherry Blossomed. So did his hair. He had chameleon eyes.

'I don't think we've met. My name's Paulton. Derek Winwood Paulton.'

'How d'you do. My name's Raine.'

'Not *the* Raine? Roland John Raine, Q.C.?'

'I'm afraid so.'

How splendid to meet you, quite splendid. I admire you so much.'

'Why?'

'Oh, come, come, Mr Raine. Don't be so modest. I'm by way of being something of a criminologist—amateur, if you like—I so admire your work. Your defence of Harry George Bundock, for instance, was worthy of Marshall Hall himself.'

'I'd rather not discuss it.'

Raine walked away and stared out of the window—out at that gaunt, empty Grandstand. Instead of being a symbol of happier days, it struck him as a gallows on which to hang the life he would never know again.

'I say, I hope I haven't offended you.'

It was Derek Winwood Paulton again.

'No, no.'

Outside, the leaves were falling. Here, at least, the trees had not been slaughtered. Dried leaves tapped on the window as if beckoning him out into the free world.

'Why are you in here?' Paulton asked.

'If you must know, I took an overdose.'

'Why, that's as common as the common cold these days. Fancy putting people away for that.'

'Yes, just fancy.'

Rather than talk about himself, Raine asked why a boy of no more than fifteen or sixteen was in this place full of grown men. He had just noticed him, reading a comic at a table by the next window. Paulton was pleased to enlighten him.

'Oh, that's young Bobby. They didn't consider him a suitable case for Borstal training. His trouble is he will masturbate in front of women old enough to be his mother.

'Dr Glazer's theory is that his mother caught him playing with himself as a child and spanked his bottom. That, of course, only intensified the delight and he yearns for the experience to be repeated.'

Paulton smiled and added:

'He'll probably be cured of it in here.'

'How?'

'He's learning the pleasures of buggery.'

'And you? What's your problem?'

'I'm so glad you asked. My trouble is I just cannot resist defecating in the street. Dr Glazer says I am one of those persons fixed at the bowel level of behaviour. He thinks that my mother once allowed me to defecate in the street when caught short and nobody else was looking and that I derived anal pleasure from it.'

'It seems to me that mothers are taking a somewhat unfair share of the blame for the oddities of human behaviour. All these Freudian pundits, of course, are men.'

'I must admit I get enormous pleasure from it.'

'And what do you think other people get?'

'Oh, they're absolutely horrified and disgusted, but that again only adds to my satisfaction. I've defecated in some of the best streets in Mayfair.'

'I believe that some burglars carry out the same practice on drawing room carpets of houses they have ransacked.'

Paulton giggled.

'And if it's an Aubusson, so much the better.'

'I think I must sit down. If you will excuse me.'

'Certainly. I've so enjoyed our little chat.

Raine sat down and closed his eyes. The Malay was still sawing at his fiddle. The long-distance runner was still running around and around. The coloured youth was still singing that black men and white men were happy together. Amid all this cacophony, one could distinguish bursts of birdsong from outside.

He kept his eyes closed because he wanted no more cosy little chats with fellow inmates. He understood that Group Therapy sessions were a regular feature of the treatment, sessions in which all the patients discussed their problems and exchanged views, a sort of confessional *en masse*. He could imagine nothing more distasteful.

'Mr Raine.'

'Yes?'

'Would you like to come along to Occupational Therapy?'

And Roland John Raine, Q.C., M.A.(Cantab), LL.B.(Hons), joined the shuffling crowd of pyjama-clad men in the basket-making class. Perhaps, he philosophised, the knowledge will come in useful when I get out of the place. Perhaps I will be able to sit on a kerb-side, calling out 'Chairs to mend'. It seemed an odd way to mend men's minds.

The next day was Saturday. In the afternoon they were allowed out to watch a basketball game between another ward and the staff. Loud were the cheers when the patients' team won.

The spectators would have poured on to the pitch at the conclusion of the game but for the fact that they were enclosed in what amounted to vast steel wire cages. However, the result of the match put everybody in a good mood and Raine wondered whether the staff hadn't thrown the game away deliberately so as to boost the morale of the patients.

In the evening a newspaper circulated around the recreation room, a Classified edition, and the men were eager to check their football pools. They had a syndicate. It would indeed be a nice irony if they scooped one of the huge prizes. It was not to be, not this week, and the anticipation and excitement gradually died away.

It was Mr Bettway who eventually turned to more mundane matters on the front page of the paper.

'I say!' he sibilated. 'Listen!'

He then read a news item to the effect that a nursing orderly at Brinstead Manor Hospital had been found murdered. He had been strangled with a pair of pyjama legs, and stripped of his own clothing. A patient, Charles Edward Oates, was missing.

So, the Quaker had 'had it away'. He was on the trot. He was out on some unfinished business.

'Does it give the dead man's name?' Raine asked.

'Yes. Nigel Fox.'

Raine heard somebody say that it served the ponce right and then realised that it was he himself who had said it, unbelievably enough. Yet he did not feel like retracting it. The dead man *was* a ponce. A ponce upon human misery. The world was full of ponces upon human misery. It was as if Oates himself was putting words into his mind and mouth.

On the Sunday there was an Anglican service of sorts in the recreation room, and the vicar from the local church mouthed holy inanities before driving home to his roast beef and two veg.

The vicar told them what lucky chaps they were to be in such good hands in their various afflictions and asked them to pray for the Royal family, reminding them that even George the Third had had to wear a strait jacket at times for his own good. He also asked them to pray for their doctors and nurses and for one, Nigel Stanley Fox of another hospital, who had died in the line of duty.

He chose the Epistle of Paul to the Galatians for the lesson. 'For the flesh lusteth against the Spirit, and the Spirit against the flesh so that ye cannot do the things that ye would. But the fruit of the Spirit is love, joy, peace, long-suffering, gentleness, goodness, faith, meekness, temperance. Be not deceived. God is not mocked. For whatsoever a man soweth, that shall he also reap.'

Then all sang *Eternal Father Strong To Save*. The Malay accompanied the hymn on his violin. The tune was quite unrecognisable.

The lusty singing gave them an appetite for the Sunday lunch of barley soup, mutton chop and swedes, followed by jelly and custard. All except Raine appeared to eat with gusto as well as relish, some with their fingers, some licking their plates clean.

It was not indigestion that kept Roland Raine awake that night. Light from a full moon filtered into the dormitory ward and he turned from one side to the other, pulling the sheets over his head in unavailing attempts to smother the crescendo of snores and even more obnoxious night sounds.

As he did one of these turns he saw the young boy, Bobby, going towards the lavatories. He was wearing only the top of his pyjamas. A few seconds later, Mr Bettway got out of bed and went in the same direction. Ten minutes later he came shuffling back but Bobby remained where he was. Another few seconds, and Paulton went towards the lavatories. He remained out there longer than Bettway. Then the coloured boy padded out there on feet as bare as the rest of his torso. He was gone perhaps half an hour.

When eventually Raine fell asleep there was still no sign of Bobby. He had no idea how many others visited the boy during the night.

He was awakened by the negro chanting about the pleasures of black man and white man together and pushing the early morning tea trolley. Bobby was helping.

That morning Raine had another session with Dr Glazer. The doctor asked him what sort of a weekend he'd had, as if he'd popped over to Paris or down to Brighton.

'I cannot say it was exactly a quiet weekend,' Raine replied, evasively. 'We sang *Eternal Father* yesterday and we prayed for you, Doctor.'

'Sometimes I think I need all your prayers,' Dr Glazer replied wrily, almost as if he meant it, and then, with a brisk change of attitude, asked if he felt like talking about his wife.

'I don't feel like it, but I will if you want me to.'

At all costs, Raine thought, I must co-operate. Otherwise I'll never get out of this cess pool.

Dr Glazer went straight to the point.

'Would you take your wife back?'

'But of course.'

'Then you still love her?'

'Of course.'

'How would you provide for her?'

'I suppose I would have to pick up the broken pieces of my career and put them together again.'

'You think that is possible?'

'It would not be easy. But other barristers have become alcoholics and made a come-back, but this is pure supposition, Doctor.'

'Yes, Mr Raine it is, but it does indicate that you really do not have to give way to absolute despair as you did last Wednesday.'

'That was not despair, Doctor. It was the most logical decision I have ever taken in my life.'

'It was logic clouded by despair.'

'Are you glad that your attempt to take your own life was frustrated?'

'Yes,' Raine lied, realising that if he replied in the negative it would have been a black mark against the prospects of his release at the end of the twenty-eight days.

'You are quite sure about that?'

Raine was aware that Dr Glazer suspected he was lying. Good barristers as a rule do not make good witnesses. Perhaps it would be better to sound not quite so certain.

'As far as I can be sure of anything at this stage, Doctor, yes, although I think the word glad is perhaps a little euphoric under the circumstances.'

'I understand precisely what you mean. Your reply to my question is yes, with reservations. Is that it?'

'Yes, that is it.'

'Until recently yours was a very successful career?'

'I could say that, yes.'

'Throughout your life, until recently, you never experienced any great rebuffs? You always achieved what you set out to do—I am not referring to day-to-day cases in the Courts—but in your own life?'

'Yes, that would be true. Perhaps that is what made me more vulnerable than I thought I was—I could not imagine anything like it happening to me. Or does that sound conceited?'

'No. Did your wife and you ever quarrel?'

'Never. We had occasional differences of opinion, of course, but never a real hammer-and-tongs row.'

To Raine, accustomed to putting questions on specific events and motives somewhat more succinctly, Dr Glazer's methods appeared to be slipshod rather than scientific, jumping from one aspect of his life to another, as if he himself was uncertain about his approach. At least, so far, he had avoided the offensive sort of questions Dr Emrys Shiplake seemed to take pleasure in.

Dr Shiplake had only succeeded in arousing his antagonism, perhaps deliberately. Dr Glazer was trying to gain his confidence, to establish a doctor/patient relationship of mutual trust essential to the successful application of psychotherapy.

Raine considered that, like Prince Hal, he had already sounded the very base-string of humility, if not degradation. He was prepared to put up with Glazer's probing pleasantries in order to get out of what Oates had so rightly described as 'a real nut-house'.

So he played his cards. He gave Dr Glazer the kind of answers he wanted. He submitted to the daily shots of vitamins. He took part in Group Therapy and Occupational Therapy, made baskets of both his boredom and his disgust, determined to play the exemplary patient. He took part in the Discussion Groups and word games that would not have taxed the intelligence of ten-year-olds. He took part in variations of What's My Line and Twenty Questions, wondering what Ministry and medicine men, yes medicine men, devised such curricula to bring light to darkened minds, but if this was what the system demanded then he, learned counsel, would play the system rather than buck it.

The doctors, the nursing staff were pleased with him. He was responding to treatment. The following Saturday, his suit having come back from the cleaners, he was allowed to go to the Saturday night dance.

5

THE DANCE WAS held in what had been the original ballroom of the old house. It had parquet flooring and pilasters. Chinese lanterns hung where chandeliers had once blazed. A spotlight hovered over the happy throng.

To Raine, they really did appear to be happy. He could not help reflecting that some debs' coming-out dances were not always as well conducted as this get-together of some four hundred men and women considered as potentially dangerous to themselves or others.

It was most proper. There was nothing comparable with Oates's lurid description of the goings-on at the Brinstead Manor dances, but perhaps mental hospitals differed as much as their patients.

Quite obviously, the Saturday night dance at Horseley was the event of the week. All the ladies wore long dresses and some of the men had dinner jackets.

Raine himself had no great knowledge of the modern dance scene, but got the impression that this was more in the tradition of Old Tyme. He would not have been surprised if the B.B.C.'s Peter West had appeared on the rostrum to MC the proceedings and count the sequins.

Smoking was not permitted on the dance floor. No lady was permitted to dance with another lady and no gentleman with a gentleman. Nurses could dance with patients of the opposite sex, but male nurses could not dance with female nurses. It was all very civilised in a nice, suburban way. An onlooker, a stranger, could not have imagined that all these relaxed people had at some time or other reached breaking point.

The only discordant note was the band itself. It consisted of male and female patients and they all sounded as if they were playing different tunes. This in no way seemed to inconvenience the dancers. Mercifully, the Malaysian with his fiddle was not included in the outfit.

Raine would have been quite happy to be a looker-on, but this was not to be. Charge Nurse Shawe, wearing a midnight blue dinner jacket, asked why he wasn't dancing. He said he wasn't very good at it.

'Does that matter? Everybody is expected to join in. Why don't you ask that young lady over there to dance?'

Raine glanced in the direction indicated by Shawe. Standing by a pilaster was a girl not much older than Jacqueline. She was not pretty and she wore glasses, gloves and was not unattractive. She was in an off the shoulder ball gown in blue taffeta and silver shoes. It was perhaps more C. & A. than Miss Selfridge but the whole *ensemble*, topped by a saucy blue bow in her hair, was quite pleasing. Raine went over.

'I'm not very good at this sort of thing,' he said, feeling frightfully staid. 'But may I have the pleasure of the next dance?'

'I kept looking in your direction,' she replied, smiling shyly, 'hoping you'd come over and ask me. And you have! Isn't that wonderful?'

'I hope you'll think the same when the dance is over.'

'But you dance divinely.'

'Young lady, I seem to have heard that before.'

'No, I mean it. Honestly I do.'

The number they were dancing to was an oldie, *Life Is Just a Bowl of Cherries* but the composer would not have recognised it. It didn't matter. It was fun.

'Have you been here long?' she asked.

'No, I'm a new boy. Or should I say a new, old boy?'

'Nonsense, you're in the prime of life.'

'Young lady, you have all the right answers. But I can't keep calling you "young lady". It sounds dreadfully pompous. My name's Raine. Roland Raine.'

'And I'm Lillian Bromley.'

'Well, how d'you do, Miss Bromley. It's nice dancing with you.'

'Mrs Bromley.'

'Oh, I'm sorry.'

'Don't apologise. Why not call me Lillian?'

'All right, Lillian. And how long have you been here?'

'Two years next October.'

'Good grief! How terrible!'

'But I love it here. It's wonderful.'

He was so startled by her reply that he trod on her silver-clad toes. He apologised again; but did she really mean what she said? She smiled up at him.

'I've never been happier in my life,' she murmured.

Then she told him her story. Her family were strict chapel-goers and her husband was of the same persuasion. Neither her father nor her mother had ever been to a theatre or cinema. They had never listened to the wireless or watched television. They never read any book except the Bible. The only musical instrument in the house was a harmonium.

'Can such families exist in this day and age?' Raine asked.

'I'll give you their address if you don't believe me. You can call on them when you leave here.'

'No, thanks. I believe you.'

'I married just to get away from the fire and brimstone atmosphere, but my husband proved to be just as narrow. I might have known it—having met him in Chapel.

'To cheer myself up during the day I bought myself a record-player and some discs. When he found out he went mad—madder than anybody in here—particularly as I'd saved up for them out of the house-keeping. It was dishonest as well as sinful, he said. He rang up my parents and *his* parents and they all came round and *prayed for me, can you imagine that?*'

She italicised her words by the very vehemence with which she uttered them. They stood still, applauding politely as the band rested. Then it was announced that the next dance would be a Veleta, whatever that was. To Raine all the numbers seemed to belong to the Victor Sylvester *genre.*

'Like to try a Veleta?' Lillian Bromley asked.

'It sounds like an Italian sweet, but I'll try it. What happened after they prayed for you?'

'Oh, from then on it became a regular thing, all of them praying to deliver me from my sinful way of life. And if that wasn't enough they got the minister in Chapel to call for prayers for me every Sunday.'

'Incredible. It's medieval.'

'Then Jack, my husband that is, found out that I was going to the pictures in the afternoon. So you know what he did? He stopped my house-keeping and turned it over to my mother-in-law for her to do *my* shopping. For me that was the last straw. I just wouldn't eat, not a thing. I mean to say, the humiliation of it all.'

They were making but token steps of a Veleta. Conversation would have been impossible if they'd essayed it any more strenuously.

'I went on hunger strike in my own home. I told Jack flat that I wouldn't touch another morsel of food until his mum stayed out of the house.'

'What did he say to that?'

'Guess what? He called a doctor in. The next day the doctor came back again with another doctor—a psychiatrist, if you please.

'They said they thought I ought to go into hospital for a little while. No mention that it was a *mental* hospital, mind you, but I don't think I would have cared if they had. I was only too glad to get out of my own home. That was the *real* mad house. Know what I mean?'

'I think I do. And you've been here nearly two years?'

'Come October, yes.'

'And you like it here?'

'I've never been happier in my life. You see, I've never known such freedom before.'

'Freedom! Did you say freedom?'

It was now Raine who italicised his words.

'I know it might sound strange to you, Roland, you don't mind if I call you Roland, do you? But look at it this way. It's Saturday night. If I was still with Jack we'd be at a chapel meeting tonight with my parents and his parents.

'I tell you, I've never had so much fun since I've been here. You hear a lot of talk about strait jackets in places like this, but in my home life I was in a permanent *mental* strait jacket. Know what I mean?'

'Yes, I think I know what you mean.'

'Everybody here is so kind, helpful and understanding. And what's more, I'm no longer in a locked ward. I'm free to walk up on the Downs every day if I want to.'

'And you really don't want to leave?'

'Shall I tell you something?'

'You've told me quite a lot as it is, but please tell me more.'

'If I wanted to leave here it would only be permitted if my next-of-kin agreed and he accepted responsibility for me. In my opinion, Roland, more often than not it's the next-of-kin who should be in here—not the likes of us. Don't you agree?'

'Yes, I think I do.'

'But gosh, I've been talking so much about myself. What about you?'

The next number was announced as an Excuse Me dance. It was another oldie called *Always.*

'Shall we try this?' Lillian asked.

'Let's,' he said.

I'll be loving you always, the vocalist breathed into the microphone. *Always.*

'So tell me about yourself.'

'Well, I took an overdose and—'

Somebody tapped Raine on the shoulder.

'Excuse me, may I take over?'

It was Mr Bettway, looking all spruced up, white moustache clipped so that it looked like the piece of cotton wool that comes out of the neck of a bottle of pills. Raine almost regretted having to relinquish his partner. He smiled at her as she tried to follow Bettway's steps which were almost as awkward as his own.

'I'll have to tell you about myself some other time.'

'Yes, please do that,' she called gaily.

Now, he thought, old Bettway will be telling her about her *libido* and *mortido*. Or will he tell her about his own problems while the band played on? Raine could hear him.

'My trouble, my dear, is that I am literally afraid of my own shadow. I am in a permanent state of anxiety which disturbs my pathological equilibrium. If I am left alone I scream like a child afraid of the dark—and I was one such child. I am suffering from general debility and loss of appetite. I have blood pressure and no capacity for sex. If my head itches I am convinced that I have lice in my hair. I have to shampoo it five, ten, twenty times a day. When Dr Glazer analysed me he elicited the fact, long since buried in my memory, that my mother once did find nits in my hair and she punished me for mixing with bad companions by whom I'd been contaminated. For the same reason I've never been able to have sexual relations with a woman. Now, if I could only find the right lady to rid me of this obsessional neurosis I'd be eternally grateful. I've asked literally hundreds of ladies to help me, stopped them in the street, but usually they call a policeman and I end up back here....'

Raine only hoped for Lillian Bromley's sake somebody would tap Bettway on the shoulder and say 'Excuse me'.

Raine found himself standing almost at the centre of the dance floor, surrounded by whirling couples. To get off the floor he had to weave his way through them and again he could not help noticing how happy everybody looked. Perhaps, he thought, ballroom dancing was the most desirable of all occupational therapies.

It was slow progress getting off the floor and by the time he succeeded the leader of the band was announcing another number.

The band leader was a jovial, silver-haired Irishman who had once been in the I.R.A. until that organisation found him an embarrassment. His trouble was that he would throw bricks through the windows of A.B.C. tea-shops. His name was Con O'Cashin and it did not take a psychiatrist to elucidate the fact that the reason he smashed so many A.B.C. windows was that the chairman of the Aereated Bread Company had once been a certain Lord Greenwood who had been commandant of the Black and Tans. It didn't mean a thing to Con O'Cashin that the erstwhile commandant of the Black and Tans was long since dead and the company had long since changed hands.

However, there was no brick in Con's hand tonight—just a bow with which he managed to make every tune sound like a jig.

Con was popular and he got a round of applause as he came to the front of the stage. He held up his bow for silence.

'And now, ladies and gentlemen,' he announced. 'Another ould favourite, a rare vintage number dedicated to our psychiatrists, one and all, God bless 'em, entitled *Can't We Talk It Over*.'

A roar of laughter greeted this sally, laughter in which the staff joined as much as the patients. Con tapped his foot, waved his bow and the band struck up *Can't We Talk It Over* in strict jig tempo.

The drummer, who doubled as vocalist, grabbed the microphone and poured out his soul.

I hate the thoughts of nights all alone,
Missing the thrills of nights that we've known,
So can't we talk it over,
Let's talk it over, dear....

There were prolonged cheers at the conclusion of this number and shouts for more, but it was time for the interval during which tea and doughnuts were served.

Raine found himself standing next to Lillian Bromley.

'How did you get on with Mr Bettway?'

'He's a sweet old man, isn't he?'

'Didn't he tell you about his troubles?'

'No, but he tried to help me with mine.'

Another girl joined them. She was giggling so much that Raine thought she was drunk and wondered how she obtained the liquor. Her name was Gertie and the others called her Gertie Giggles. When she wasn't giggling there was an expression of serene happiness on her face. It would appear that life for Gertie really was a bowl of cherries—and double cream—even in this place.

She had been at Horseley West since the age of puberty and was now a most nubile nineteen. She wore a print dress with revealing neckline and mini-skirt. Like most of the patients, she derived pleasure from discussing her own enforced hospitalisation.

'My trouble is I just can't stop laughing,' she said. 'Isn't that a scream?'

'What do you find so funny?' Raine asked.

'Oh, everything. You, me, Lillian, Dr Glazer, the staff. Everybody taking themselves so seriously when it's all a load of cock really, isn't it? Don't you agree?'

'And what did you find so funny in the outside world?'

'Well, I was just a schoolkid when my parents put me in here. I was just about to take my A levels and I'd already done O. I was very good at O.'

'But what did you find so funny?'

'Everything, everybody. The other kids, the teachers, my parents. I used to laugh till I wet myself. I still do.'

'I would not have thought that was sufficient reason for having you locked up in a mental hospital.'

'Well, it proves one thing,' Gertie replied between giggles 'The world doesn't laugh with you when you laugh. You can cry your eyes out and that's okay, that's fine, that's normal, but just keep laughing and you're a nut case, that's me.'

'I don't believe it,' said Raine. 'Any more than I am.'

'I'm what they call a hebephrenic,' she said.

'What on earth is that?'

'The word comes from Hebe.'

'The cup bearer to the gods?'

'You're bang on, Mr Raine. So I have all the symptoms of a lush, behaving as if I'm pissed when I haven't had a drop. They say I have bizarre behaviour patterns.'

'And what about your parents?'

'Oh, they're a nice normal couple living in the suburbs. Very respectable. I haven't set eyes on them since they dumped me in here. Isn't that a scream?'

'I don't think it's screamingly funny.'

'Ah, there you are. You haven't my sense of humour. Hello, there's the band starting up again. Shall we dance?'

'I'm not very good at it.'

'Never mind. I don't expect Fred Astaire.'

They went on to the dance floor, she giggling with every other step. The tune was *Puppet on a String.*

'Isn't this fun?' said Gertie. 'All of us out of our tiny minds? Dancing cheek to cheek?'

'I would say that it is one of the less unpleasant aspects of the place.'

'My, we are formal, aren't we, Mr Raine?'

'Would you prefer me to be a little more—let us say—bizarre?'

'Just plain bizarre—or Marks and Sparks bizarre?'

She thought this so funny that she ceased dancing, clinging to him, convulsed with laughter, the other dancers swirling around them, the spotlight hovering.

In that moment there came a blood-curdling scream. The scream was followed by a thud.

One of the women patients, an idiopathic epileptic, was in the throes of a seizure. In falling, her head hit the parquet flooring. Blood oozed around the dancers' feet.

The band played on. Epileptic fits were not an infrequent occurrence at Horseley West and it would have been a pity to waste precious dancing time.

A number of nurses, male and female, ran to assist the stricken woman.

This sent Gertie into another paroxysm of laughter. She must have been aware of the shocked expression on Raine's face, because she attempted to justify her manic merriment.

'You must admit this hospital is equipped with all modern cons,' she said. 'Including hot and cold running nurses.'

Again she exploded with laughter, falling about this time, colliding with other dancers.

Raine walked away. He could take no more of her company. As he did so he reflected that this weird young woman was about the same age as his own daughter. Perhaps he had something to be grateful for.

The following week Dr Glazer told him that he was to be transferred to an unlocked ward and that he would be free to walk in the grounds. He suggested he might like to take a walk over the Downs. This was a measure of the confidence Glazer had in Raine.

Raine decided to take a walk across the Downs that very morning. He hoped that he would meet Lillian Bromley. The morning was fair and the sun was high, but a breeze dishevelled his hair. High in the sky larks wheeled.

He kept expanding his lungs with the crisp, clean air. He felt good. Life, after all, was worth living. Now when he looked up at the Grandstand he did not feel that it was as empty as his own life. Soon both would be full again.

Distantly, he heard the rattle of hooves on the firm going. He felt so exuberant that he was quite confident he could have jog-trotted the entire Derby distance himself, one mile and a half and a few yards. He smiled at his own conceit. He really would have looked crazy, a middle-aged man, with windswept, greying hair, panting all alone around Tattenham Corner.

A car rustled up alongside him, a Doctor sticker on the windscreen. The occupant was a woman.

'Want a lift?' she asked.

Why not? he thought. It would have been churlish to decline the offer. Besides, she was quite attractive. She wore a Hermes headscarf and a cherry-red trouser suit. Rather gay attire for a doctor, he thought, but then why should a woman doctor be expected to dress as sombrely as her male colleagues.

'That's kind of you.'

She flicked the door open and he got in. He could not see the colour of her eyes because she was wearing dark glasses, but the wisps of hair on the nape of her neck were titian.

She drove fast and with assurance, keeping only her left hand on the wheel. He noticed that she wore a thin, platinum wedding ring and a square diamond.

'Would you mind lighting me a cigarette. You will find some in my handbag.'

The handbag, between her feet and the gears, was also Hermes. Alongside the packet of cigarettes was a gold Dunhill. He lit a cigarette and handed it to her.

'Thank you. Aren't you smoking yourself?'

'I'm afraid I don't.'

He was aware of the fact that he must have sounded a bit staid because she apologised for asking him, a non-smoker, to light a cigarette for her. Adding to this discomfiture, she flipped the cigarette out of the window.

'I say, I hope you didn't throw that away just because I don't use them?'

'Not at all. I never take more than a couple of puffs. It's a filthy habit anyway.'

Glancing at the speedometer, it occurred to Raine that she must be in a hurry to get back to the Hospital, but when he saw a sign-post pointing to Ewell he realised that she was driving in the opposite direction. She must be attached to one of the other fourteen in the district.

As if reading his thoughts, she announced that she was making for Belgravia and would that suit him? He said it would. Did he know London well? Reasonably well. Yes, he was a Londoner.

'My name's Raine. Roland Raine.'

'Well, how d'you do, Mr Raine. I'm Eileen Prepend. Oh, dear! What is that silly man trying to do?'

With not a little skill she managed to avoid the driver who had shot out of a side road without warning and then, also without warning, attempted to execute a U-turn. She put her foot down hard.

'Best to give dolts like that plenty of distance,' she said. 'Now, that fellow really should be in Horseley West.'

'Are you a doctor at Horseley West, Mrs Prepend?'

She tilted her chin and relaxed against the seat in order to give full vent to her laughter.

'A doctor! I'm like you, a patient running away from the place.'

'How did you know I was a patient?'

'I saw you at the dance on Saturday night, all wrapped up with that bitch, Lillian Bromley.'

'Why do you describe her as a bitch?'

'She tried to poison her husband, didn't she?'

'I wasn't aware of that, but from what she told me about him it would have been justifiable homicide if she had succeeded.'

'You surely don't believe everything you're told, do you? Not in that place?'

'On the contrary.'

'What you mean is—you don't believe anybody?'

'I did not say that.'

'Well, she was certainly giving you an earful last Saturday night—and were you lapping it up!'

'How could you tell?'

'From the expression on your face.'

'The lights were fairly dim.'

'Not as dim as you looked.'

'Thank you for the compliment, Mrs Prepend.'

'Oh, don't mention it.'

'Would you like another cigarette?'

'I'll tell you when I want one.'

'I presume you have borrowed this car?'

'I think the charge would be "taking possession of and driving away without the owner's consent".'

'Do you know much about police court charges?'

'No, but that's the sort of thing one reads about.'

'You must have been very anxious to get away.'

'Well, who wouldn't? How about you?'

'I wasn't planning to run away.'

'No? Well, look. If you want to go back I can drop you at Morden Station. You can get a bus from there. Or walk.'

'I have suddenly decided that I have no wish to go back.'

'In that case you can light me another cigarette.'

He did so.

She thanked him and then asked, 'What were you in for?'

'I took an overdose. How about you?'

'I kept getting obscene telephone calls, threatening ones as well. I complained to the police and the 'phone people. Nothing was done about it. They refused to intercept the calls because they said I was imagining them. Then when I had a breakdown I was persuaded to go to Horseley West—voluntary. And do you know what Dr Glazer said?'

'No.'

'He said I was suffering from auditory hallucinations. Can you believe it?'

'Yes. I can now believe almost anything.'

'Three weeks I've been there and this morning I decided I'd had enough. That place really was driving me cuckoo.'

'But if you'd agreed to go there for twenty-eight days you had only another week to go.'

'Yes, but I knew bloody well that Dr Glazer wouldn't let me go after the twenty-eight days were up.'

'Why not?'

'Because, my dear Mr Raine, he wants to fuck me.'

'How do you know.'

'Oh, be your age! A woman always knows.'

'Sometimes a woman just imagines.'

'Not Eileen Prepend.'

'Where are we heading for?'

'Disaster probably.'

With this remark she put back her head and laughed as if she had said the funniest thing of the year.

'Seriously though, will Belgravia suit you?'

'I'll take Belgravia,' he said.

'Actually,' she said, 'I think it's Chelsea, but don't let's quibble.'

'No, don't let's quibble.'

'That punk Glazer.'

'What about him?'

'He said I was suffering from diminished sexual control. So you know what I told him?'

'No. What did you tell him?'

'I said "Thank God for that, Dr Glazer. That means I'm normal".'

Raine could not resist smiling.

'Did you have wife trouble?' she asked.

'Sort of.'

'You make it sound just a bit too casual. Tell me about it.'

6

Eileen Prepend abandoned the borrowed car alongside the house in Knightsbridge which had once been the home of Hudson the Railway King and is now the French Embassy. She put a five-pound note into the glove compartment, explaining that it was to pay for the petrol and the possibility of a parking ticket.

'Although a doctor should know better than to leave his keys in the ignition outside a mental hospital,' she said, winding up the window before getting out.

Raine could not help feeling that her gesture with the note in the glove compartment was both flamboyant and overtly meticulous. He had always been dubious of people who made that sort of display of their own honesty, feeling that it concealed a deeper dishonesty, but of late he had found himself shedding some of his prejudices.

They walked round Wilton Crescent in the direction of her mews house off Chester Square. The house had a pastel green door and wire baskets of trailing geraniums over the shuttered ground floor window. Scarlet petals decorated the cobble-stones. She smiled up at the plants.

'You've been weeping tears of blood for your absent mistress, haven't you, my poppets?' she said to them.

Perhaps, he thought, she really is mad.

'There's two bottles of Pol Roger in the kitchen,' she said. 'Be an angel, and put them both in the fridge, there's a darling. I can't bother with all the paraphernalia of putting them in an ice bucket. I feel like celebrating.' She hurried upstairs.

Raine did as requested. Then he paced up and down between the kitchen and the front door. Presently she called out to him to bring one of the bottles upstairs. He managed to find a silver tray and suitable glasses. Then, with a napkin over his arm, he ascended the stairs.

'Come in!' she called out.

She was sitting on a *pouffe* in her bedroom, wearing a transparent *négligé* in white chiffon. The red trouser suit had been tossed on to the bed.

He extracted the cork without making even a suggestion of a pop.

'Ah,' she said. 'A true *sommelier*, eh?'

'Not really,' he replied, handing her a filled glass. 'It so happens I used to open half a bottle every morning before going to work.'

She raised her glass.

'Well, cheers.'

'Cheers.'

'What's the matter?' she asked. 'You look ill at ease?'

'Do I? I'm sorry.'

'Oh, don't be sorry. Just relax.'

She was unpinning her hair and it cascaded over her shoulders. He could now see that her eyes were hazel.

'Would you be more at ease if you took your clothes off?'

'It's an idea,' he said.

'If you're shy—there's a dressing gown in the wardrobe.'

He took his jacket off and tossed it on to the bed.

'I'm not shy, but this just happens to be a trifle unconventional, that's all.'

'Oh, Jesus Christ Almighty!' she said. 'Here we are, the two of us, just out of a nut house, and you talk about being unconventional.

'What's the matter with you? Missing the Occupational Therapy?'

'Can I refill your glass?'

She slid off the *pouffe* on to the floor, opened her legs and stroked herself.

'No, fill this.'

He took the rest of his clothes off.

He did not exactly undress with alacrity. Although this woman was perhaps fifteen years younger than himself she made him feel like an inexperienced youth being seduced by someone old enough to be his mother. Moreover, as seduction it wasn't particularly alluring. It did not quite suggest the Song of Solomon. She was neither a Rose of Sharon, nor a lily of the valley. Come to that, he could not quite see himself as a bunch of myrtle between her breasts.

Certainly nobody could accuse Eileen Prepend of frigidity. It was more than apparent that her life was governed by what the psychiatrists called the Pleasure Principle, and not by the Reality Principle. There was no doubt about her *libido* being in the ascendant. Dr Glazer certainly had not exaggerated when he told her she was suffering from diminished sexual control.

She pulled Raine down over her and he heard her teeth grind. Then she nipped the lobe of his left ear. Her heels pressed into the small of his back as she jerked convulsively. She inserted her ringed finger into his anus.

'Oh, Jesus, it's beautiful, it's fucking beautiful. Oh, oh, oh, it's beautifully fucking. Don't stop, don't stop. Not yet, not yet, not yet. Oh, ooh, ugh. I'm coming.'

Her face contorted, eyes closed as if she was suffering unbearable pain.

After a while she sat up on the *pouffe* again, sat there hands clasped round her knees, looking down at him.

'Now do you give a damn about that bitch of a wife of yours?'

It was quite obvious that Eileen Prepend regarded almost every other woman as 'a bitch'. As he did not answer she repeated the question.

'No,' he lied.

She reached for her cigarettes and lit one. This reminded him of Veronica. Veronica used to smoke in the bedroom. It was a habit that he had never cared for, but he had never asked her not to do so.

'You're the strong, silent type, aren't you?' Eileen declared rather than asked.

'What do you mean?'

'You're not very demonstrative when you fuck.'

'I suppose not. Have you any complaints?'

'No, but I like to know my partner is enjoying it as much as I do.'

'I can assure you here and now that I was.'

She tried to mimic his tone.

'Is that the truth, the whole truth and nothing but the truth?'

'It is, so help me, God.'

She twisted around, reaching backwards and upwards to stub out the cigarette in the ashtray on the bedside table. Then she affected a little shiver.

'Let's get into bed, shall we?'

In bed she began to giggle.

'Know something?'

'What?'

'They're doing Group Therapy at Horseley now.'

'So they are.'

'We've got our own Group Therapy, haven't we?'

'Yes.'

'Or maybe they're doing psychodrama.'

'What is that exactly?'

'Haven't you had psychodrama? Oh, darling, you haven't had treatment at all.'

'But what is it?'

'It's another form of Group Therapy.'

She reached down to the floor for another cigarette and lit it.

'You all take it in turns to act out what's troubling you,' she said. 'In my case, I had to repeat all those nasty 'phone calls I'd had, the actual filthy words, mind you, and even try to imitate the voice. It's a bit of a scream really, but I don't think it's quite nice, do you?'

'I should imagine that it's damned unpleasant.'

'It's quite funny watching the others though.'

'I would have thought it just as acutely embarrassing to watch as to make an exhibition of oneself. I cannot imagine what useful purpose it can serve.'

'They say it helps to relieve tensions.'

She reached out to stub the cigarette from which she had taken one puff.

'But we've got our own way of relieving tensions, haven't we, darling?'

'Yes.'

'That Lillian Bromley, I could have died with laughing at her in psychodrama.'

'Why?'

'Well, she acts her trouble out by going down on her knees and imitating all her family praying to her. Talk about male and female impersonations! Of course, you know who she thinks she is, don't you?'

'No.'

'The Virgin Mary, of course. That's why she imagines she sees her family praying to her.'

'That's not the way she told it to me. She told me her parents and parents-in-law prayed *for* her, not to her.'

'Well, a few prayers in her direction wouldn't be out of place, I can tell you.'

'She seems to like it there.'

''Course she does with the head man poking her every other day. No wonder she thinks she's the Queen Bee and the Virgin Mary rolled into one.'

'If what you say is correct I cannot see how she can delude herself into believing that she is the Virgin Mary.'

'Oh, but that's easy. She thinks Dr Glazer is the Holy Ghost and she's really being fucked by her Heavenly Father. See what I mean?'

'Well, not really.'

She laughed.

'I tell you, some of those women at Horseley are quite shameless. The things they get up to! You'd be shocked, really you would, Roland.'

'I used to think I was past being shocked.'

She laughed again and explored him beneath the sheets.

'And how's my unshockable heavenly father. My he's limp, isn't he? Did he like Eileen's cunt? I think he deserves a kiss.'

She threw the sheets back, positioning herself to indulge in fellatio. As she did so the telephone pip-pipped. She ignored it. The 'phone stopped before she did.

She lifted herself up and went into the bathroom. He heard water running. He saw countless reflections of himself in the mirrors on the ceiling over the bed and in the long pier glass by the wardrobe. It was as if he was in a Hall of Distorting Mirrors in some fairground. That grotesque, unclothed man could not be himself. Never. Roland John Raine, Q.C., M.A.(Cantab), LL.B.(Hons), never looked like that fellow and he would certainly never have behaved like that fellow.

Eileen called to him from the bathroom. She wanted more champagne. He took it into her. She was up to her shoulders in a bubble bath. She had tied her hair up again.

She handed him a large oval of mauve soap, raising herself out of the bubbles, but not quite like Venus emerging from the waves.

'Soap my breasts, darling.'

She made mewing sounds of delicious appreciation as he did so, gyrating first one shoulder and then the other, holding herself up by clasping her hands around the back of his neck. He found it quite tiring and was pleased when she said that was enough.

Then she stood up, turned her back to him and bent over, presenting the shiny orb of her bottom to him.

'Kiss the bubbles out of my arse, darling.'

He was glad that he could not catch any mirror's reflection of himself in this ludicrous activity. Eileen Prepend didn't think it ludicrous. She moaned with pleasure.

'That's lovely, that's good. Open it up, darling. Tongue right inside that little rose-bud. Ooh, ooh, that's beautiful. I'm coming, darling, I'm coming.'

Suddenly she jerked upright and rested her head in her arms against the bathroom wall. Then slowly she turned to face him, legs apart.

'Now my clitoris.'

From the bedroom came the pip-pipping of the telephone again.

'Don't stop, darling. It's one of those obscene calls. They must know I'm back. They go on all the time. All the time, all the time.'

In her complete abandonment to her own sensual delight her voice became drowsy as if from sleep, then slowly she lowered herself into the bath again.

'Get in the bath with me, darling.'

Ten minutes later they were both on the bed, wrapped in Turkish towelling. The telephone started again.

'Let it ring,' she said.

'Who do you suppose is responsible for these calls?'

'My husband.'

'But surely you would recognise his voice?'

'Oh, he doesn't make the calls personally. He pays other people to make them.'

'But why?'

'Because he wants to get me out of this house, that's why.'

'Perhaps I'm simple, but why does he want to get you out of the house?'

'Because it's worth a bomb, darling, and he needs the money. He'd have been in here like a shot when I went to Horseley, but I took the precaution of having the locks changed.'

Raine found himself wondering what sort of a man could be married to a woman like Eileen Prepend and, as if she had guessed his thoughts, she supplied the answer.

'He's a professional gambler, darling. That's what broke up our marriage. Do you know he would sooner spend all night at the Victoria Sporting Club than come home to bed with me? Can you believe that?'

Raine did not tell her so, but he could believe it. It occurred to him that Mr Prepend might find a night of Black Jack less exhausting than a night in bed with Mrs Prepend.

'Gambling,' she continued. 'It's a disease, that's what it is. Why don't they put all the gamblers into mental hospitals?'

'Perhaps that's the reason they've got fifteen around Epsom,' he said. 'As a matter of fact, there is a compulsive gambler in Horseley. He's making a book on the November Handicap.'

'I wish they'd put Bernie in there. Then maybe I'd get a bit of peace.'

Perhaps, Raine thought, it was Bernie Prepend who wanted a bit of peace. Once again it was as if she had known what was in his mind.

'You don't think I'm one of those nymphomaniacs, do you?'

'No, of course not.'

'Well, you're wrong, darling. I am. I can never get enough of it.'

'In that case, why didn't you let Dr Glazer have his way with you?'

Eileen Prepend arched her body and then collapsed in what could only be described as uncontrollable laughter.

'You really are square, aren't you?' she said eventually, then tried to mimic his voice. ' "Why didn't I let Dr Glazer have his way with me?" Why don't you say what you mean? Why don't you say why didn't I let him fuck me? I'll tell you why. Because I decide which man fucks me. Not the other way about.'

'And when did you decide that I was going to?'

'When I saw you this morning up on the Downs, palely loitering. You looked so sad and lonely.'

'Your impression was quite mistaken. I was feeling better than I'd felt in years.'

At this moment the front door bell chimed, one, two and three, doh, ray, mee. Eileen went to the window and looked down through a chink in the heavy curtaining.

'I thought so. It's the Gestapo.'

'What do they want?'

'You, I should think.'

'Why me—and not you?'

'Darling, I was a voluntary patient. You had been committed there.'

'Why should they look for me here?'

'Oh, be your age! I thought you were at the criminal Bar. Two patients disappear, also one of the doctors' cars. It is found five minutes from my address. It doesn't take a Sherlock Holmes to work it out.'

The bell chimed again.

'One would think they had something better to do,' he said.

'You would, wouldn't you.'

'Of course, they might want to question you on the subject of taking and driving away a car without the owner's permission.'

'You'd still think they'd have something better to do. I bet there's a bank being robbed in Knightsbridge right this very minute.'

'However, one really can't blame the police, I suppose. They don't make the Law.'

'No, it's the likes of you who do that.'

'That isn't entirely true.'

They heard a powerful engine start up and the sound of the police car moving off.

'They'll be back,' she said.

She began caressing him again, but the physical attractions of Eileen Prepend had already begun to pall on Roland Raine. Consequently she elicited little or no response.

'I know what you want,' she said, getting out of bed.

'What is that?'

'Some food. No man can perform on an empty stomach.'

She began to dress and fifteen minutes later he heard the front door close. She had previously called out that she was going to Harrods' Food Hall and told him not to answer the 'phone.

He thought he heard the key turn in the lock from the outside. In which case he was locked in, but he could not be quite sure. Perhaps he, too, was now suffering from auditory hallucinations. Such was the world he had been existing in recently that it was difficult to differentiate between reality and what was not real.

Nothing was what it seemed to be, not even oneself.

It did seem that he had exchanged a public mad house for a private one. Ought he to dress and try to get out of the private one, get himself taken back in a police car to Horseley West to play Animal, Vegetable, Mineral games and mental Scrabble. But almost certainly it would be going back to a locked ward again or, as they so nicely called it, a secure ward.

A secure ward for insecure people.

But places like Horseley West were for people who could not cope with an unhappy life situation. Thanks to Eileen Prepend he had got away from the place. It would be admitting defeat to go back, just as it had been admitting defeat in swallowing those barbiturates in St James's Park. And that was the ultimate in abject failure.

There was not much doubt about it that Eileen Prepend was slightly mad, and no doubt at all that she was uncommonly coarse and vulgar, if not depraved. He would have been horrified if Veronica had ever behaved as this woman had behaved. Horrified and disgusted.

The sex life he had enjoyed with Veronica had never been anything but what is regarded as conventional, or normal, but who is to decide what is normal in sex? In comparing Veronica with this strumpet, Eileen Prepend, and to the latter's disadvantage, he had an uncomfortable feeling that he might have stumbled on the unpalatable truth, the not-to-be-admitted truth. Could it be that Veronica was a sister under the skin to Eileen Prepend, that she had the same sort of uninhibited desires deep down? If so, Dr Emrys Shiplake had been on the right line with his offensive questions about their sex life.

It would go a long way towards explaining Veronica's hitherto inexplicable decision to abandon both husband and daughter for a man entirely without refinement, a man with whom she need have no shame or self-consciousness. Had not Bundock's own wife been a whore on whom he had ponced in his less palmy days?

Yet what right had he got to presume that Eileen Prepend was mad because of her somewhat startling behaviour with a complete stranger? Again he reminded himself of the two words inscribed on the Temple of Delphi: Know Thyself. Two words that Carlyle had dismissed as an 'impossible precept'. It had certainly been borne in upon him in these recent days that indeed he did not know himself or, at least, he did not know himself as well as he thought he did.

By the same token, what right had the Dr Glazers of the world to presume that they knew mentally sick people better than they knew themselves? When the famous Dr Hunter nearly succumbed to the effects of a heart attack he said that his life was in the hands of any rascal who chose to annoy and tease him. Surely the same threat could apply to one's own sanity?

Raine was pondering these somewhat morbid questions when Eileen arrived back. She was so laden that she had taken a taxi to the corner of the mews.

'I didn't take it right inside in case you were scared it was the police again,' she explained.

He wanted to say that he wasn't scared of the police. He was apprehensive about the prospect of being carted back to Horseley West, but he wasn't scared of the police.

However, Eileen Prepend cooked such an excellent meal, *truite amand*, that he felt a bit of a cad in having entertained derogatory thoughts about her, let alone having doubted her sanity.

He gathered that at the age of seventeen she'd been a Lido girl and had learned the art *culinaire* when staying with a French family. It is perhaps a sad reflection that it is not always the most virtuous who best qualify for the *Cordon Bleu*.

She did not remove the shutters from the dining room—'in case those bogey men come nosing around again'—but she lit candles. He was really enthusiastic about the food, not being able to remember the last time he'd had a decent meal.

The wine was excellent too. A Montrachet. She really was a good hostess in the best sense of the word. More than ever, he chided himself as a bloody ingrate. Why should he complain if she was a bawd in the bedroom?

'Nothing wrong with the wine is there?' she asked anxiously.

'Good God, no. It's superb. Why do you ask?'

'The expression on your face.'

'I'm sorry. It must have been involuntary. I was just ticking myself off.'

'About what?'

Raine held up a finger.

'That is between my analyst and me.'

'I suggest you forget about Horseley. That's all over and done with. All you have to do is to stay in the clear until the twenty-eight days are up. Make plans. In the meantime you can stay here until you're on your feet again.'

He demurred, made excuses. The one thing he ought to do was to trace his daughter. Eileen Prepend scoffed at this. Why this sudden decision? He had made no attempt to trace her before. Anyway, any girl with the starry-eyed guts to take on a self-imposed task of trying to improve the lot of meths drinkers would be more than able to take care of herself. Besides, supposing he did succeed in tracing her? What would it avail either her—or him? She was not likely to abandon her crazy crusade until she realised the hopelessness and uselessness of it herself.

There seemed to be a good deal of sound commonsense in Eileen Prepend's arguments but, to use a modern vulgarism, he was uneasy about the prospect of getting shacked up with her, and—to use another—it just wasn't his scene.

'No, Eileen. I really can't impose on you.'

She gave a husky, throaty laugh, her chin tilting back, mouth wide open and showing her dentures, upper and lower.

'Roland, you are quaint at times. It's the first time I've heard it called imposing. I like a man around the house. Or haven't you noticed?'

'Yes, I have and I'm flattered. But why me?'

'Why not?'

He felt pretty stupid because he did not know how to answer the question. He could think of nothing to say.

'Well,' she said, 'I never thought I'd see a barrister lost for words.'

'Barristers do not usually find themselves in situations like this,' he said. 'Or in mental hospitals, if it comes to that.'

'No, of course not. They think it only happens to other people. Just what makes barristers think they're so high and mighty?'

'They don't, really.'

'They're either high and mighty or toffee-nosed.'

'I must admit that some of us have not got exactly endearing qualities but that surely applies to all professions. Doctors, for instance.'

'I take people as I find them.'

He was tempted to say, yes—he was sure she did, but thought she might take offence and so remained silent over his brandy.

Eileen Prepend was an enigma, more so than most women. She had an undoubted charm. She was quite good-looking. She was not uneducated. She knew about good food and wine. She was accomplished, yet withal remained *monstreuse.*

Anyway, what alternative was there to staying here? Use her telephone to ring up an old friend? He remembered the last time he'd done that. He'd telephoned Reggie Paignton, Q.C., who'd been at Cambridge with him.

'Hullo, Roland, old scout!' Reggie had greeted him. 'How nice to hear from you! Wondered where you'd got to. What can I do for you?'

And then that distinct flattening of the voice as he said, 'A bed for the night? Sure thing. I'll just check with Mavis.'

A long pause and then ... 'Hello? Look Roland, I'm awfully sorry about this, but we've got the children home from school and they've brought a couple of chums with them. So we've got a pretty full house. Any other time, of course, only too glad to have you. Do keep in touch.'

The word had got around that he'd become a hopeless alcoholic and it was always the wives who thought up the excuses. Or was it? Were the men hiding behind the women's skirts?

Being a man himself he liked to think it was the house-proud women who did not want to have their homes sullied by the presence of a man who had hit the skids. He had to confess that, by and large, he did not like the wives of his brother barristers, tweedy women who drove their hubbies to the railway station in the morning and collected them again at night, lest they went astray. Taking it in turn to drive each others' children to and from school, having Tupperware coffee mornings and Weightwatchers' sessions, once-a-week golf and bridge in the evening.

Perhaps he was unreasonable. How did he expect civilised women to conduct their lives? He knew that Veronica shared his opinion of them, but then, look what had happened to Veronica.

Between them, Raine and Eileen Prepend finished a bottle of brandy, both getting rather high. The more Eileen drank the coarser she got, particularly in reminiscing.

'It was on my twelfth birthday that I took my Girl Guide's oath to be pure in thought, word and deed,' she recalled. 'Then on the Sunday the Scoutmaster, an old man of at least thirty, got me alone in the church hall and on the pretext that my shoe lace was undone, he went down to me.

'It was one hell of a shock, but I got my first lovely, shuddering orgasm. I shall never forget it as long as I live. He could have put his pole up me right there and then.

'He got two years later for indecently assaulting little girls. I'd have given him his Pathfinder's Badge and the Explorer's.'

'And today he wouldn't have been imprisoned. He'd have been sent to Horseley West,' Raine said.

'Well, you must admit it's a more enlightened society today.'

'With reservations, yes.'

'At least at Horseley they would have tried to cure him.'

'How?'

'Well, they would have tried to explain things to him. The ultimate in sex is not just self-gratification but to drive your partner crazy with joy. That was what he was trying to do to me, and he succeeded.'

'How do you know that is the way it would have been explained to him? It seems to me that would encourage him, not cure him.'

'Because that is the way it was explained to me.'

'You told them about it?'

'They asked me.'

'So they took you back to your twelfth birthday? They must have covered a lot of ground in three weeks.'

'Oh, it wasn't this time. It was the time before.'

'You've been in Horseley West before?'

'Didn't I tell you? Oh, I forgot. The last time was years ago and that time it wasn't voluntary.'

'You'd been bound over on some charge on the condition that you had psychiatric treatment?'

'That's right. I was charged with indecent assaults on young boys. I don't see what was indecent about it. I was educating them, showing them how to do it instead of drawing it on a blackboard, like teachers do, which is downright disgusting if you ask me. The psychiatrist didn't put it that way, though. He said I was revenging myself on the male sex for what the Scoutmaster had done to me. He'd got it all wrong. I was showing my appreciation for what the Scoutmaster had done to me by returning the compliment, this time for the benefit of the male sex. Do you get my meaning?'

'I'm afraid it's all a little too involved for me. Or perhaps I've had too much brandy.'

'Then perhaps we'd better put out the candles and go to bed.'

'Yes, I think that's a good idea.'

They both began puffing at the candle flames and it was some minutes before they succeeded in putting them all out.

7

TO WALK OUT of a mental hospital, indeed any hospital, into twenty-four hours of debauchery requires not a little physical as well as mental acclimatisation, and the following morning found Raine in a debilitated state. Eileen took his temperature and said it was a hundred and three. She told him to stay in bed and turned the bedside radio on for him. Then she went downstairs to make some coffee.

On the radio there was a brief news item to the effect that a verdict of wilful murder by some person or persons unknown had been returned at the resumed inquest on Nigel Stanley Fox, a nursing orderly at Brinstead Manor Hospital.

There was no mention of Charles Edward Oates. So Charlie Boy was still at large, at large on his 'unfinished business', and this unfinished business included a confrontation with Harry George Bundock, although actually it was none of Oates's business at all.

A psychotic like Oates would never see this. Oates was capable of mindless and motiveless murder, the most difficult type of murder case to solve. Raine was not particularly concerned about Harry George Bundock's skin, but was afraid that Veronica might get involved in some unpleasant way.

It was true that Bundock was a big man in the underworld and that Oates was small fry. Bundock would almost certainly have strong arm men, or 'minders'. Even so, Oates was not to be underestimated. He was capable of biding his time until he could get Bundock alone.

In the paranoid world of gangsters there is a phrase—'to make a name for himself'—which is unique, inasmuch as it applies to small-timers who succeeded in inflicting some grievous bodily harm on one of the big shots. In this way the small-timer acquires kudos. That alone would be sufficient to motivate Oates into having a go at Bundock, quite apart from any animal-like devotion he might feel for Raine.

Oates was already in serious trouble. Raine felt it to be his duty to get to him before Oates could add to the tally—as if one murder wasn't enough. How he would make contact with Oates was not quite clear in his mind, particularly as the police hadn't succeeded.

Meanwhile, Raine decided to telephone Veronica to suggest to her, without explaining why, that she should get out of town for a few days. He hoped she would have the good sense to take his advice.

Raine did not know Bundock's telephone number, but was fairly certain that he could obtain it from Scotland Yard who would most assuredly have that gentleman's line tapped day and night, even if it was supposed to be against the law.

Relations between the Yard and himself had been a little cool since he'd got that Not Guilty verdict at Bundock's trial, but there was a young detective in the Special Crimes Squad with good reason to be grateful to Raine, who had been indirectly responsible for getting him a Commissioner's Commendation. Detective-Sergeant Dick Mantle would know Bundock's telephone number.

Detective-Sergeant Dick Mantle knew more than Bundock's telephone number. He had news for Raine. Red hot news.

'Mr Raine,' he said. 'Before you go any further I think you ought to know that your wife has left Bundock.'

It was like the beat of a drum, the crash of cymbals, the blast of bugles rising to a crescendo unbelievable. For a couple of seconds Raine could not speak.

'Are you there, Mr Raine? I said your—'

'Yes, I heard you. Thank you. Where is she?'

'Just a second, I have the address here. Mrs Raine is at 59b Brushfield Street, Spitalfields, E1.'

'Thank you.'

Raine replaced the 'phone on the bedside table. The address did not sound particularly salubrious, but that was unimportant. The main thing was that Veronica had come to her senses at long last and had left Bundock.

He slid out of bed and hurried into the bathroom. He shaved

with an electric razor which presumably had belonged to Mr Bernie Prepend.

As he came out of the bathroom fully dressed he saw Eileen coming up the stairs with coffee. She stared at him.

'Where do you think you're going?'

'Spitalfields.'

His reply convinced her that he must be demented. Perhaps, in a subdued and non-medical way, he was.

'Get straight back into bed, darling. I'll call the doctor.'

'Eileen, I've seen enough doctors in the past week or two to last me a life-time. I'm sorry, Eileen, but I really must go. It's urgent.'

'Rubbish. You've got a temperature of a hundred and three. You must be crazy. Spitalfields! What's urgent at Spitalfields?'

'My wife is there.'

Eileen put the coffee down and folded her arms.

'You're lying. What would your wife be doing at Spitalfields?'

'I don't know, but that's where she is.'

'How do you know?'

'Scotland Yard told me.'

'Was that who you were 'phoning?'

He nodded.

'You must be mad, 'phoning Scotland Yard. Don't you know you're wanted. You're just as much a fugitive as a murderer. You've escaped from a mental hospital. For all they know you might be violent. Don't you realise your description's been issued to all police stations?'

'The Yard didn't say anything about it.'

'Of course not. They just want you to walk into a trap.'

'That's nonsense. They had no idea I was going to telephone. The Yard has got more important things to do than set traps for people who've walked out of mental hospitals.'

'What about the squad car that came nosing around here yesterday with three cops in it? You said yourself you'd have thought they'd have something better to do.'

'Even so, I can't imagine Scotland Yard going to the lengths of setting a trap for me in an outlandish place like Spitalfields.'

'Then what's your wife doing in an outlandish place like Spitalfields? Shelling peas? Picking gooseberries?'

Suddenly, he had the answer to that question, although he didn't tell Eileen. The area around Spitalfields Fruit Market was one of the worst in London for meths drinkers. It was Metholand. Now he knew why Veronica was there. She had found Jacqueline.

'I don't know what she's doing there, Eileen. But I intend to find out.'

'Now I know you must be a nut case. You really should be in a padded cell to protect you from yourself. A no-good bitch who leaves you for a rotten crook, she's not fit to—'

'Eileen, you're going just a little too far.'

'Going too far!' Eileen Prepend screamed. 'I haven't gone far enough yet. I took pity on you, picked you up when you hadn't got a penny to bless yourself with, gave you food and shelter and my own bed, then the minute you hear where that cow is you go running back to her. What sort of a man are you and what sort of a woman do you take me for?'

'Eileen, I'm not ungrateful to you.'

'Oh, don't give me that smarmy law courts talk. Like shit, it's elliptical. And you're a shit, a pimp. Okay, get out of here and don't come crawling back to me next time she walks out on you. Good riddance.'

He said nothing. In the face of this tirade there was nothing one could say. What few shreds of dignity he had left he must try to keep. So he walked down the stairs, while she remained on the landing shouting abuse at him.

In Chester Square he had to hold on to the railings for fear that he would slither to the ground. Perspiration streamed from him. His knees wanted to buckle beneath him. As he clung to the railings he realised that he would have to walk all the way to Spitalfields.

It took him five minutes to reach the other side of the Square. At this rate of non-progress it would take hours. He reckoned that it would take a fit man at least a couple of hours.

He did think of boarding a 9 bus at Knightsbridge to Aldgate and explaining that he had no money, giving his name and address, but what address could he give. Horseley West Hospital? And he had no proof of identity.

It took him three-quarters of an hour to reach Hyde Park Corner.

His heart nearly stopped when a police car cruised to a stop alongside him, but with relief he saw that it was merely held at the lights.

He took the underpass to Green Park and thence to St James's Park. By this time it was nearly midday. He sat on the grass under a tree. He heard the *pipeau* of sparrows and other bird calls. It was as if he had just emerged from a self-induced nightmare.

Yet when he got uneasily to his feet and started to walk again he realised that the nightmare was still with him. Crossing Trafalgar Square he was within inches of getting knocked down by a 15 bus. The driver leaned out of his cabin and yelled at him.

'You shouldn't be allowed out on your own, mate.'

Raine plunged into the hurly-burly of the grubby Strand, once called by Disraeli 'the First street in Europe'. At Aldwych he held on to a sandbin for support.

He felt that he just had to have a drink of water, he felt so faint, then remembered the drinking fountain at Lincoln's Inn Fields.

He had the iron cup pressed to his mouth when he heard somebody call, 'On the wagon at last, eh, Roland?'

It was Reggie Paignton, Q.C. He had the reputation of being a bit of a wit. He was wearing his starched white bib and was obviously on his way from the Law Courts to lunch.

'That's funny,' said Raine. 'I was thinking of you only yesterday.'

'We often think of you,' said Reggie. 'When are you coming down to see us?'

'Oh, one of these days, one of these days. I say, Reggie, you couldn't lend me a pound, could you? I've come out without any cash.'

'That makes two of us, Roland. I never carry cash in these mugging days—just credit cards. Tell you what though—pop into my chambers and see my clerk. He'll fix you up.'

'Thanks,' said Raine. 'Don't worry.'

He let the iron cup clang back into the iron basin and continued on his way. Traffic sounds were magnified tenfold. The streets seemed to be ten times more crowded than usual. Every other person seemed to be colliding with him. He walked as if in a drunken stupor.

Another half hour saw him at Ludgate Circus. Twenty minutes later he was sitting on the steps of St Paul's Cathedral. Pigeons walked gingerly towards him, as if they had followed him from St James's Park. It was here that Veronica and he had first heard Verdi's *Requiem*.

He must have looked ill because when he tried to get to his

feet a young woman gave him a hand, saying 'Ups-a-daisy' as if speaking to some incapacitated child.

'Thank you,' he said. 'Thank you.'

'Are you all right?'

'Oh, yes. I'm fine, thanks.'

Cheapside was so crowded he might have been walking against an emerging football crowd. He sat down on one of the seats outside the Royal Exchange and again by the statue to George Peabody.

His snail-like progress was such that he became increasingly desperate, desperate with the fear that by the time he reached Brushfield Street both Veronica and Jacqueline would have left there.

He could not imagine Veronica wanting to stay for long in an area as squalid as Spitalfields and she would almost certainly do her best to persuade Jacqueline to move elsewhere. It was also conceivable that Jacqueline might agree now that her mother needed her. Jacqueline had an intense loyalty to her mother.

She had, of course, been deeply hurt when Veronica had gone off with Bundock, but never a reproachful word had escaped her lips. Raine was convinced that Jacqueline's decision to go off to work among the meths drinkers had been her way of assuaging her own intense grief.

By the time he reached Liverpool Street Station the evening rush hour was commencing. The walk had taken him all day. Yet only yesterday morning, when he had been taking deep breaths of the fresh air up on Epsom Downs, he had felt that life was still worth living, forgetting of course that a stroll across Epsom Downs on a pleasant autumn morning has no relation to urban life, except as an escape from it.

Presumably that was why nearly all mental hospitals had been built on the outskirts of towns rather than in them.

In an endeavour to escape the crush of commuters in Broad Street and Bishopsgate he went into the Great Eastern Hotel and sat down. A waiter emerged. Did he require tea? No, he lied. He was waiting for the bar to open, but could he have a glass of water? Of course, sir.

Veronica and he had stayed here *en route* for Harwich and Holland in tulip time.

He had taken so much alcohol yesterday—champagne, Montrachet, cognac—and so much of it remained in his system that the water had a slightly stimulating effect. He now felt strong enough to complete the last phase of his trek. It was but a short walk to Brushfield Street. The sight of meths drinkers asleep or semi-comatose in doorways all over the place indicated that he was heading in the right direction.

Raine managed to make it a much longer walk by getting lost in the labyrinth of side streets and alleyways between Middlesex Street and Bishopsgate, so that eventually he approached Brushfield Street from the direction of Commercial Street with its fancy goods and Oriental fashion warehouses, Pakistani rag trade emporiums and Far Eastern Banks.

Number 59b Brushfield Street was an early nineteenth-century house due for demolition. It was dusk as Raine approached it, and he saw a man hurry out towards a car parked at the other end of the street, get in and drive off. Raine was almost certain that it was Oates. In fact, he tried to increase his pace but before he even reached 59b the car had turned the corner.

The front door had one of those heavy knockers from an age when craftsmen took pride and pleasure in ironwork. Raine lifted it and let it fall several times. There was dried vomit on the pavement outside and an empty British-type sherry bottle.

What was incongruous in these surroundings was the latest E-type Jaguar parked outside. Surely it could not belong to Veronica?

As he waited for some response from within the mean little house, Raine watched a lanky, purple-visaged man with long grey locks picking over a heap of rotten apples in the opposite gutter, and cramming the selected ones into his quite toothless mouth. He wore an obscure tartan tam-o'-shanter cap over his matted hair, a brass-buttoned army greatcoat *circa* 1914 and sandals on sockless feet. The neck of a bottle jutted from one of the greatcoat pockets.

'You lookin' f'r Jackie?' he called out.

'Yes. There's no reply.'

'She ain't there, cobber. She's down Old Ford way. Why don'cher go up'n wait?'

'How do I get in?'

'Jes' push the door, cobber. It ain't never closed.'

'Thanks.'

He did so, shivering at the thought of Jacqueline keeping an ever-open door in this reeking jungle. The door thudded behind him.

The stairs creaked as he went up.

On the landing he stumbled, not from fatigue, but because apparently there was somebody sleeping on the floor. Raine presumed it was a meths drinker who had crawled in for the night. Little or no light penetrated the landing window, for it was largely covered over by a piece of cardboard, a pane having been broken.

On the principle of letting sleeping dogs lie, Raine made no attempt to awaken the recumbent figure, but pushed open a door on which he could dimly discern Jacqueline's name and that of the voluntary organisation for which she worked.

Hopefully he flicked the electric light switch just inside the door, and a ceiling light came on from an unshaded bulb of no more than 25-watt strength.

The room was almost as spartan as a nun's cell. There was a divan against the wall and one Windsor-type wooden chair, and against the window was a small table on which were several large sandwich loaves, some tins of Fray Bentos corned beef, some packets of margarine or butter and a café-size tin of Nescafé. There was also a large tin of powdered milk, beside which were a number of thermos flasks.

It did not take a Sherlock Holmes nor even a Dr Watson to deduce that this was the table at which Jacqueline prepared midnight snacks for the monstrous army of utterly debased no-hopers who infested the district. There was a gas stove in one corner, on which it seemed that some milk had boiled over. There was faded linoleum on the floor and what looked like butcher's muslin across the window. Raine opened a cupboard which served as a wardrobe and recognised some of Jacqueline's clothes hanging inside. But there was no sign of Veronica's.

As he thought, Veronica would never have stayed in a depressing hovel like this for very long. Although mother and daughter were very much alike, Veronica differed from Jacqueline in that she liked what are called 'creature comforts'. Veronica had never been one for slumming, although it might be argued that she had gone sexually slumming when she went off with Bundock.

He sat down on the Windsor chair, elbows resting on his knees, chin in his fists, reconciling himself to the fact that all he could do was await Jacqueline's return. He was famished and the array of loaves and tins of corned beef on the table tempted him to cut a sandwich. He did this as best he could with a butter knife, not being able to find a bread knife, and then sat down again, taking ravenous bites at the 'doorstep' sandwich. It was, he thought, somewhat staler fare than Eileen Prepend had prepared for him, and there was no Montrachet to wash it down. He did not feel like coping with the processed milk.

Well, Eileen Prepend had been wrong in asserting that Scotland Yard had laid a sinister plot to trap him in Brushfield Street. He was quite prepared to believe that all police stations were circulated with descriptions of escapees from mental hospitals, and that it was the duty of the police to apprehend such escapees, but it was hardly a matter for the Yard.

However, he was more concerned about Jacqueline than for his own situation. He had never approved of her starry-eyed sojourn among these debased creatures, but until this evening he had never actually seen the surroundings in which she worked, nor the meths drinkers themselves.

As though he had committed some crime, Raine was filled with remorse. He had failed Jacqueline as a father, although deep down he knew that no parental authority would have stayed her from doing what she wanted to do once her mind was made up. Even so, he could not rid himself of the guilt feeling.

He decided that it was high time to assert himself, both as a person and as a father. He had been acquiescent for too long in the face of adversity and what the psychiatrists liked to call an unhappy life situation. Belatedly, perhaps, it was now time for him to change that unhappy life situation, to refuse to accept it spinelessly, as he had been doing for so long. He was reconciled to the fact that nothing he could say would induce Jacqueline to abandon her misplaced good Samaritanism, but the thought of these befouled creatures actually sleeping on the landing outside her room horrified him as much as the realisation that it was common knowledge in these parts that she had an ever-open door. It was a miracle that she had not been strangled in her bed. There was not even a telephone in the room for her to use in summoning help if threatened.

His first step would be to get rid of that fellow on the landing. He got up and went to the door.

'Hey, you!' he shouted. 'Get out of here.'

The recumbent figure did not stir. Raine pitched his voice even louder as became a man who had once served in the Honourable Artillery Company.

'D'you hear me. Get out of here.'

Raine lost his patience. The pent-up tensions of the past week or two, the submerged resentments of being subjected to humiliation after humiliation in the name of medication, came welling to the surface. He prodded the man with his toe.

'Get out! You can't sleep it off here. Get out!'

There was still no response and so Raine bent down to shout in the man's ear. The shout died in his thorax.

No wonder he had been unable to find a bread knife. It had been plunged into the back of the man on the floor.

Moreover, now that a thin ray of light from the 25-watt bulb penetrated the landing from under the door he could see that the victim was far too well-dressed to be a meths drinker. It was Harry George Bundock.

Now Raine realised that the glimpse he'd had of Charlie Oates had been no hallucination. It also explained the E-type Jaguar outside. It belonged to Bundock. He must have followed Veronica here and Oates must have followed Bundock.

But where was Veronica?

8

IT WAS POSSIBLY foolish of Raine to have removed the knife. Certainly as a barrister he should have known better, but none of us, unless specifically trained to cope with emergencies unlikely to be met with normally, knows how we would act in a like situation. After all, it was conceivable that Bundock's life was not yet extinct.

The lining of one of the dead man's pockets was hanging out. So it would seem that Oates had robbed as well as murdered him.

Raine wrapped the knife in a tissue he had found in the room and was about to leave in search of the nearest police station when the front door was opened and Jacqueline came in.

She stood there, framed in the open doorway, his beloved Jacqueline whom he had not seen for nearly three years, looking lovelier than ever in spite of being clad in faded jeans and suede boots. Her caramel coloured hair was drawn back in a pony tail.

'Daddy!'

She rushed up the stairs and he hurried down towards her so that they met midway, almost colliding. They held each other very close for what seemed an eternity.

'Jacqueline.'

'Daddy.'

'Let me look at you,' he said.

But Jacqueline had pulled away a little and was looking at what he was holding and then she looked into his face, her limpid green eyes searching.

'Jacqueline, something terrible has happened.'

She looked past him, up the stairs.

'Yes,' she said, very calmly. 'So I see.'

'Jacqueline, you don't think I—'

'Daddy, of course not. It's unthinkable. We'd better go round to the police station and report it.'

'I was just on my way,' he said.

'I'll come with you.'

It was disconcerting for Raine to realise that his daughter was far calmer than he. Perhaps her life among the meths drinkers had conditioned her to shocks, whereas his lifetime at the criminal Bar had not hardened him, at least not to the same extent.

As they went down the stairs together, however, he realised that she was not as cool and calm as she appeared to be. She was trembling like a leaf.

'I suppose I'd better lock the door,' she said.

'Yes, I was going to talk to you about that. In this part of the world—'

'Please, Daddy, don't nag at me.'

Her hand was trembling as she turned the key. Then she turned to him, trying to smile.

'I'm sorry,' she said. 'I didn't mean to snap at you. Let me take that. It won't be so conspicuous in my bag.'

She took the wrapped knife from him and placed it in the sling bag she wore over her shoulder, one of those fabric satchels such as are used by people distributing pamphlets or handing out free girlie mags.

They walked along Commercial Street together, father and daughter re-united after three years, neither of them knowing quite what to say, neither of them feeling as composed as their outward appearance would suggest.

Traffic thundered past them, silver Freightliners and red buses, packed legions of Mr Cubes from Silvertown, shoals of fish fingers from Hull, sheet glass for Hackney and newsprint from Dartford.

'You know, Jacqueline, I could very easily be the number one suspect in this terrible business.'

'Daddy, don't joke, please!'

'I'm not joking, darling. I'm serious.'

'If anybody is to be blamed, it's me,' she said.

'How can you say that?'

'I went away to help uncaring strangers when it was Mummy and you who really needed me. I could have kept you together.'

'Darling, you are being less than fair to yourself. Your mother and I were adults. Perhaps it was we who did not give you sufficient love.'

'Daddy, you both gave me everything. Perhaps you gave me too much. I felt as if I was being smothered by love. You both gave me so much love I was frightened by it. I was afraid of becoming a spoiled brat.'

'That, my darling, was a groundless fear. It was not in your nature.'

'But what does one know at seventeen?'

'Probably a little less than what one thinks one knows. How is Mummy?'

'Very unhappy.'

'She didn't stay with you?'

'No, she took one look at my place and moved into the Great Eastern.'

'Good God!'

'What's so astonishing about that?'

'It must have been telepathy. I went in there earlier this evening to rest my weary feet.'

'She's been round to see me every day, trying to persuade me to give up what I've been doing. Actually I had already decided to do so. I was getting so disillusioned, but I hadn't made up my mind what to do. Tell you what, let's both go round and see Mummy later on, shall we?'

'I'd love to, but does she want to see me?'

'I'm sure she does, but she won't admit it. Mummy's a bit like me.'

His mouth puckered.

'I would say that you're more than a bit like Mummy.'

'And I think she feels rather ashamed, as indeed I do. We both let you down, badly.'

'Oh, Jacqueline, for heaven's sake, let's stop reproaching ourselves, shall we?

'I was there when Bundock arrived to try to persuade her to go back to him. He certainly went the wrong way about it. He was absolutely vile. The things he called Mummy! I couldn't stand it.

'You left?'

'Yes, I left. Here's the police station.'

'Good. Let's go in and get this business over and done with.'

They went up the steps and the sergeant on duty greeted

Jacqueline, she being well-known locally for what was considered misguided Good Samaritanism.

'Hullo, Miss Raine.'

'Hullo, sergeant. May I introduce my father. Daddy, this is Sergeant Brand, a good friend of mine.'

'Pleased to meet you, sir. Your daughter's a brave girl but, dear me, she worries the life out of us. What can we do for you, Miss Raine?'

'We've come to report a murder.'

'Oh, crikey! One of them meths drinkers, I suppose?'

'As a matter of fact, no.'

'I discovered the body, sergeant,' Raine broke in. 'The dead man is a Harry George Bundock. You may have heard of him.'

'That bleeder. Excuse my language, miss. Well, we won't weep no tears over him. All the same, murder's murder. You'd better see the Superintendent.'

Sergeant Brand lifted a telephone. Jacqueline was unbuckling her shoulder bag. She placed the knife on the sergeant's desk.

'This was in the body. And here is the key to 59b Brushfield Street, where you will find the body.'

Sergeant Brand, on the 'phone, nodded.

'Hullo, sir. I've got Miss Raine with me—and her father. They've come to report a murder. I'd better send them up, hadn't I? Yes, sir. Right away.'

The sergeant came with them to the stairs.

'First floor, second door on the right.'

'Thank you.'

The sergeant's eyes followed them up the stairs. He shook his head. He'd be very surprised if them meths drinkers were not behind it. A nice girl like her shouldn't be mixed up with that filthy lot. A pity her father hadn't arrived on the scene long ago. It was a mercy she hadn't been murdered herself.

Not so long ago, the sergeant mused to himself, there'd been a fire at Gardner's Corner which had completely gutted the empty store. In the shell of the building firemen had found charred corpses of meths drinkers who'd assumed squatters rights to the premises, lit a fire to warm themselves and had died in it. Best thing that could have happened to them, he reckoned. Burn the lot of them, that's what he'd do, burn 'em like lice in a mattress.

Chief Detective-Superintendent Clipstone stood up to greet Raine and Jacqueline.

'Hello, Jacqueline. Good evening, Mr Raine.'

'Good evening, Superintendent,' said Raine. 'Haven't we met before?'

'Indeed we have, sir. Do take a seat. I was a young detective sergeant giving evidence for the first time in a murder case and you gave me a hard time in the box because I'd admitted to picking up the gun and muffing the prints on it.'

'Well, now it's your turn to give me a hard time, Superintendent. I've done something similar.'

'Tell me about it.'

When Raine had finished his story the Superintendent nodded and suggested that they both might like to write out statements in the office next door.

Meanwhile he 'phoned his opposite number in the Murder Squad at the Yard.

'Hello, Tommy. Clip here. Oh, not so bad. How's yourself? Good. Well, it looks as if we're in business. There's been a murder round the corner from here in Brushfield Street. Victim a certain Harry George Bundock of whom you have doubtless heard. At least, that's what I'm told by the man who discovered the body, Mr Roland Raine. Yes, that's right, the Q.C.

'Right. I'll see you round there with your team. Brushfield Street runs off Spitalfields Market. Number 59b. Tell your driver to look for Percy Dalton's Peanut Warehouse. It's just past there. Yes, nuts to you too. G'bye. See you.'

Then he picked up the 'phone again and asked for Sir Barnes Hilton, Professor in Pathology at the London Hospital.

Having spoken to the pathologist and given him the address, Clipstone ordered his car. He called in to see Jacqueline and Raine on his way out to the scene of the crime.

'Oh, Jacqueline,' he said. 'I don't suppose you'll want to stay at Brushfield Street tonight.'

She told him she would prefer not to, and that she could stay at Old Ford with Mrs Billing, one of the local social workers.

'Good, good,' said Clipstone. 'And you, Mr Raine. Where will you be staying?'

'Do you know,' said Raine quite truthfully. 'I hadn't given it a thought.'

'You won't be staying where you stayed last night?'

Raine felt almost tempted to laugh.

'No, I will not be staying where I stayed last night.'

'I can fix you up with a place for the time being, Daddy,' said Jacqueline.

'Good,' said Clipstone again. 'Perhaps you wouldn't mind giving me a ring later, Jacqueline, to tell me where your father is?'

'Yes, I'll do that.'

'Oh, and there's just one more thing. Where is your mother staying?'

'At the Great Eastern Hotel. We're going round to see her later.'

'Ah, that's nice and handy. Would you mind asking her to give me a ring, if not tonight, first thing tomorrow morning.'

'Yes, I'll do that.'

'Thank you. Goodbye for now, and thank you both for calling.'

And Chief Detective-Superintendent Clipstone went down the steps to his car for his rendezvous at the scene of the murder with his opposite number, Superintendent Tom Gretton of the Murder Squad and Sir Barnes Hilton, pathologist, plus various supernumeraries like finger print men and photographers.

Jacqueline and Raine signed their statements and left.

'Let's go and see Mummy, shall we?' said Jacqueline.

'Yes, let's do that.

'After all,' Raine added. 'Somebody had better break the news to her—before she reads about it in the newspapers.'

'I don't think it's going to break her heart,' said Jacqueline.

'Don't you think we ought to telephone first? Mummy might not want to see me.'

'Daddy, she wants to see you more than any other person in the world, but she won't admit it. She needs you and you need her. We all need each other. If we could only wipe out the past.'

'Unfortunately we can't, but we can always make a fresh start.'

'Daddy, I'm going to grab that taxi. You're walking as if you're dead on your feet.'

'I feel rather like that.'

As they got into the cab Jacqueline said, 'We'll make Mummy buy us dinner at the Great Eastern. I bet you haven't had a thing.'

'I had the biggest corned beef sandwich in the world,' he said.

Jacqueline appeared to be in command of the situation. On

arrival at the Great Eastern she told her father to go into the bar, pressing a pound note on him.

'I'm sure you could do with a drink.'

'I certainly could. Shall I order one for you?'

'A Coke, Daddy, thanks.'

He winced.

'That is something I refuse to order, even for you, Jacqueline.'

'Oh, all right, you're just being the same difficult old Daddy. I'll have a dry sherry, then.'

'That's better. Shall I order something for Mummy?'

'That would be a nice idea, but I'd better give you some more money. A pound goes nowhere these days.'

'Jacqueline, you can't afford to buy rounds of drinks in British Rail hotel bars.'

'It's only once in a while. In any case, I'm not broke, Daddy. Don't you remember you bought an annuity for me maturing on my eighteenth birthday?'

'So I did,' he said vaguely. 'So I did.'

'And as I spend almost nothing on myself it's practically intact.'

'What shall I order for Mummy?'

'I've an idea. Why don't we all have champagne?'

'It'll cost the earth.'

'Daddy, this is a re-union party. Let's be reckless. You go in and order a bottle. I'll ask for Mummy at the desk. I won't say you're here. I'm just longing to see the expression on her face when she sees you. She'll swoon, believe me.'

Raine did not really think that the occasion called for champagne, but knew that Veronica liked it as much as he did. So he asked for the wine list.

There were three glasses on the table and the champagne in an ice bucket when Jacqueline came back. She was alone. He expected her to say that Mummy would be down in a few minutes, that she was making her face up or doing her hair or something like that, but she didn't.

'Daddy,' she said. 'Mummy's checked out and she hasn't left a forwarding address. What do you make of that?'

'I don't know,' he said. 'I really don't know.'

9

JACQUELINE HAD FOUND accommodation for her father in a hostel in the Mile End Road, not far from where Captain Bligh had lived in the days when the district was much favoured residentially by masters of sailing vessels. Hope House was for professional men who had encountered adversity or setbacks somewhat late in life, and had been unable to cope with them. Here were middle-aged first offenders; here was the bank clerk who had been detected with his hand in the till; there was the accountant who had over-cooked the accounts; there the solicitor who had speculated with his client's money; and here the struck-off doctor alongside the defrocked cleric.

To call it Hope House was a bit of a misnomer, because for most of these people there was no hope. It was a house of silent men, each keeping himself to himself, seeking neither sympathy nor the camaraderie of companions in distress. All they had in common was disillusionment.

Most of them had accepted poorly paid employment, beneath their status. Others received a form of national assistance known as supplementary benefit, although what it was supplementary to wasn't quite clear. They paid most of it to the hostel for their keep.

There was a sitting room and in it that universal panacea, the television set. Around this sat the inmates as if participating in a wake for their own lives. There was complete non-communication as well as complete indifference to what passed as entertainment on the bland screen.

Among them sat Raine. He sat there because there was nowhere else to sit.

None of the residents was permitted to go to bed before lights out.

There was a bookcase but he had not bothered to explore the contents.

He was not ungrateful to Jacqueline for fixing him up with accommodation here, but she could have had no idea how incredibly dreary it was in this front room overlooking the Mile End Road, opposite a mustard-coloured high-rise block of council flats.

He missed the news item about the murder in Brushfield Street because at that moment he was told the Warden wished to see him in his private sitting room.

Raine was only too glad to get away from the sepulchral atmosphere of what was known as the Residents' Lounge.

He was reminded of the line in *Ulysses* about the nightmare from which one never awakens.

The Warden was surprisingly young, with a cheerful, easy-to-get-on-with attitude. A smiling, handshaking young man. His name was Ricketts and he had been a probation officer. He ran Hope House with the help of his wife, Gwen, who had also been a probation officer.

'Do sit down, Mr Raine.'

Raine sat. His face was expressionless, unable to return the sympathetic smile. He had no desire for sympathy, no wish for any heart-to-heart chat. He just wanted to be left alone.

'I hope I didn't interrupt a favourite programme, Mr Raine?'

He shook his head. He did not wish to be rude, but neither did he wish to speak or exchange inane pleasantries.

'The point is, Mr Raine, that you should not be here at all.'

'Oh.'

'No. Much as we'd love to have you here.'

Raine winced at the young man's effulgent politeness.

'You see, I gather you're a Horseley West patient and as such you should be returned there.'

And as such I should be returned there. I am a parcel that has gone astray. A parcel with its wrapping loose.

A parcel in which the time-bomb of my mind has exploded, leaving only paper and string with tangled knots. As such I am to be returned to the Lost Parcels Office at Horseley West, the Mount Pleasant of mental hospitalisation. There they will unravel the knots and tie me up again in a new wrapping. Then I will be re-addressed—to where?

'I'm surprised that Superintendent Clipstone did not realise you should have been returned to Horseley West,' the Warden continued. 'Much as I would like to keep you on here I dare not. Do you know that I could be fined five hundred pounds for giving aid and shelter to a patient who has been committed to Horseley West under the 1959 Act?'

Ricketts was impressed with the dramatic implications of having Raine on the premises. Raine was not so impressed. He'd had enough of drama. He shook his head. No, he did not know that any person giving him shelter was liable to a fine of five hundred pounds.

'So, I'm afraid, Mr Raine. You'll just have to go back. There's a police car here from Epsom.'

Raine was almost tempted to smile. Charlie Oates was still at large and he—Raine—was to be taken back to hospital in a police car.

'I feel rather like Al Capone,' he said, as he got into the car.

None of the police officers replied. They all stared at the road ahead. Three policemen and a big car to take him back to hospital. Am I mad? Or the world?

Night had fallen and with it an autumn chill, although it was warm in the big white car with blue lamp on the roof. Eddies of refuse were blown along the gutters. Skirting Spitalfields Market, the car was suddenly bathed in a roseate hue from the flames of a bonfire.

It had been lit by the meths drinkers on a piece of waste ground, with fruit boxes, newspapers and any other combustible rubbish. About thirty of the methos stood around it, warming different parts of their anatomies, their already empurpled features dyed an even more lurid hue, some blood orange, others carnation, some with faces resembling the centres of ripe pomegranates. It was impossible to tell male from female.

These, Raine thought, are the uncaring strangers that Jacqueline left home to help, a thankless, unrewarding task if ever there was one. Those who had their backs to the bonfire stared sullenly at the passing police car. It was like passing an outpost of Hell itself.

Ash from the burning debris was carried aloft and then fell like Old Man's Beard all around, spattering and rendering even more grotesque the ragbag of Metholand gathered together around their own funeral pyre. Compared with this scarlet-visaged crew Caliban was an Antony, he mused, the Witches of Endor beauty queens.

Could they, he wondered, have suffered any catastrophes worse or even comparable with those which had befallen him? He doubted it.

Yet they were free. Free to bring about their own demise slowly, loathsomely, filthily. Free to light bonfires in the streets for warmth and to illuminate their living death. The very stench of them seemed to penetrate the car.

It was amongst these that his own daughter went the rounds with sandwiches and flasks of hot drinks, which would have to do battle with the poison that was rotting their guts, poison bought with money supplied by the Ministry of Health and Social Security, the same Ministry under whose aegis he was being conveyed to a locked ward.

The dormitory ward was in darkness when he was handed over and the police car rustled away, but he saw dim forms padding to and fro. A voice that he recognised as Paulton's whispered 'Welcome home!'

The following morning it became apparent to Raine that he was in considerable disfavour with the authorities. No doctor sent for him and the nursing staff eyed him almost reproachfully. He had betrayed their trust. He had brought a stigma upon this mental healing institution. Come what may, there would be no question of his being released at the end of the statutory twenty-eight days, presuming that he was still in their care.

He was not asked to attend either Group Therapy or Vocational Therapy and for this he was grateful. In the recreation room things were very much as before. The long-distance runner kept long-distance running. The Malay boy provided the same ear-splitting accompaniment. The old man still played hopscotch and the one-time hotel doorman still gave two-finger whistles and yelled 'Taxi!' as if it was the end of a ball.

Mr Bettway sibilated his greetings and told him it was obvious that his *mortido* was in the ascendant.

'This is the tension which activates all our destructive urges, my dear chap,' he said. 'From it stems all hatred and blind anger from which, in turn, stems both murder and suicide. Both are acts of aggression over which you had no control. It is unfortunate perhaps for you that your suicide bid failed whilst the murder succeeded, but I wouldn't worry too much, old chap. I daresay Dr Glazer will speak up for you in Court as unfit to plead, even though you did blot your copy book by running away. They won't send you to prison, but Dr Glazer will ask to keep you under his care and you'll probably be out of here in five years, or ten at most.'

'Thank you,' said Raine. 'Now will you please leave me alone?'

Mr Bettway wagged a roguish finger at him, smiling indulgently as he said, 'There you go again, letting the *mortido* get the upper hand. Why don't you give your *libido* a chance?'

Why don't I give my *libido* a chance? Why don't I fly to the moon? Why don't I sing *Land of Hope and Glory* standing on my head? Why don't I do handsprings up and down the ward? The terrible thought struck him that dotty, sibilating old Bettway might be right.

He felt Jacqueline's arms round his neck and heard her fierce whisper, 'Daddy, you mustn't give up. Promise me you won't give up.'

He looked out of the window at the big white Grandstand. He no longer heard Veronica's voice shouting the winner home.

There really was nothing to shout about. Where could she be?

He tried not to think of happy days he had enjoyed with both Veronica and Jacqueline, because he knew Dante Alighieri's *'Nessun maggior dolore, Che ricordarsi del tempo felice, Nella miseria.'*

Truly he could echo that there was no greater sorrow than to recall happy times in misery.

He tried to eat Sunday lunch, not wishing to undergo the final humiliation of forcible feeding, but when he pushed his plate aside a new inmate, who had already finished his own helping, began scooping the remains from Raine's rejected plate, using both hands to cram the slimy potatoes and veg into his bursting maw.

Paulton explained to Raine that the newcomer was being treated for gluttony.

'Quite disgusting, isn't it?' he said. 'Glazer's theory is that when he was a small child his mother snatched his food away if he didn't eat it up quickly enough. As a result he gobbles up everything in sight as quickly as he can for fear of going hungry.'

'Does Dr Glazer discuss *all* the case histories with you?' Raine asked.

'No, dear boy, but I keep my ear to the ground.'

'It strikes me that Glazer has an outsize mother hatred complex.'

Sunday brought the same vicar and the same lesson: 'For the flesh lusteth against the Spirit, and the Spirit against the flesh so that ye cannot do the things that ye would. But the fruit of the Spirit is love, joy, peace, gentleness, goodness, faith, meekness, temperance. Be not deceived. God is not mocked. For whatsoever a man soweth, that shall he also reap....'

Then all stood to sing *There is a Green Hill Far Away*.

After the service the vicar sought him out and asked if there was anything he could do. Raine shook his head. The vicar was a good man according to his lights, however, and tried to offer words of comfort. Bettway was not the only one, it seemed, who presumed Raine's guilt.

'Remember our dear Lord,' he murmured. 'He was oppressed and he was afflicted, yet he opened not his mouth; he is brought as a lamb to the slaughter, and as a sheep before her shearers is dumb, so he openeth his mouth.'

Raine thought the situation could have been put a little more tactfully. Nevertheless, he thanked the servant of God for his kindness. It was all very well, but he knew there was not the least likelihood of his being charged with the murder of Bundock.

Or could he be so sure? The police were a long time getting round to arresting Oates. It made Raine feel just a little uneasy. On the other hand, he could not imagine anything happening that could worsen his own situation.

On the same Sunday afternoon he was informed he had a visitor. He almost expected it to be a Scotland Yard officer, questioning him about his statement, but to his delight it was Jacqueline.

She had been shopping the previous day and had dressed up for the occasion, wearing a green and white polka dot dress with a green straw boater and matching shoes, handbag and gloves.

She looked so pretty that Raine felt his eyes tingling. Twenty years ago it could have been Veronica herself. She was even wearing a perfume that her mother had worn at her age.

'Any news of Mummy?' he asked.

Jacqueline shook her head.

'Not a word. I'm worried. I can't understand it.'

'What does Superintendent Clipstone say?'

'He asked me if I'd like him to issue an appeal to her to come forward as she might be able to help them with their enquiries. I said no.'

'Quite right. Can't you imagine how the newspapers would play that up?'

'I can, Daddy, I can. By the way, Superintendent Clipstone is furious with the Warden of Hope House for taking it upon himself to ring the Epsom police and get you put back here.'

'I can't say I'm very pleased with that young gentleman either.'

'I'm sorry, Daddy. It's my fault.'

'Will you stop blaming yourself for everything, Jacqueline? You've been absolutely marvellous.'

'It wasn't very bright of me to get you fixed up at Hope House, though. Mr Ricketts is one of those career do-gooders who leans over backwards to obey the letter of the law.'

'Let's sit over by the window, shall we?'

'Yes, let's.'

He tried to laugh, gesturing at the cordless dressing gown and striped pyjamas.

'I'm sorry they don't issue us with Sunday best here.'

'Oh, I've left a Daks suit for you at the office, Daddy, and some shirts and underwear. I got them at Simpsons yesterday.'

'Darling, that's marvellous of you. But heaven knows when I'll be able to wear them.'

'You'll be wearing them tomorrow.'

'I don't understand you.'

'Superintendent Clipstone has told me I can secure your release from the hospital by applying to a judge in chambers, and he's fixed it for tomorrow. All I have to do is to say I will be responsible for you. After all, I am your next-of-kin after Mummy. Mr Clipstone will support the application too.'

'Jacqueline! That's wonderful. Let me give you a hug.'

'Daddy, everybody's looking.'

'I don't give a damn. Let them look.'

He was proud of this impulsive, starry-eyed daughter of his. Green, starry-eyed and as impulsive as her mother. He laughed out loud, slapping his own knee.

'So I'm to be placed in your care, am I?'

She nodded.

'Provided the judge consents.'

'Who is the judge? Do you know?'

'Lord Fife.'

'Oh, old Drum and Fife! He's a nice old boy.'

'Let's hope he'll be nice tomorrow.'

'He will be. I remember in the days when we had a death penalty he was as nice as pie to a client of mine he was sentencing to death. Almost apologised.'

'Daddy! Don't, it makes me shiver.'

'Time's up,' said one of the male nurses.

Time's up. Just like prison on visiting day. Except this was more bizarre and more pathetic. Men in prison wore neat uniforms. Here the inmates had to greet their visitors in unsightly pyjamas and cordless dressing gowns, and wearing slippers that flapped as they walked. In prison they knew when they would be released. Here, none knew for certain. For some it would be never.

When Jacqueline left, Raine stood at the window waving to her as she walked down the drive under the tall poplars which seemed to make obeisances to her, long arms tossing her their last leaves. She kept stopping to wave back. Then she was gone.

Raine felt like singing. Perhaps the nightmare was ending after all.

'That was a nice young lady,' said Mr Bettway.

'Thank you,' said Raine. 'It was my daughter.'

'How nice for you. Nobody comes to see me.'

'I'm sorry.'

'Oh, don't be sorry for me. I'm being discharged next week.'

'Really! I'm pleased to hear it. That's grand. What are you going to do?'

'I'm setting up as a consultant psychologist.'

'Well, I hope you get lots of clients.'

'Oh, I will. I will. I've done it before.'

'How do you set about it?'

'Oh, I put small ads in all the national newspapers. Consultant psychologist cures Blushing, Shyness, Stammering, Inhibitions, Lack of Confidence.'

'Doesn't one have to have a degree, have had training?'

'My dear Raine, I've been having free training here and elsewhere for years. I print the names of all the hospitals I've been in on my card. Most impressive, you know.'

'I'm sure it is.'

Raine turned away, not wishing to get involved in a long confabulation with Bettway. As he turned away the old man playing hopscotch slipped and fell flat on his face.

'Can't you look where you're going?' he screamed at Raine. 'Now I've got to start all over again.'

Nearly everybody laughed, and Paulton, mocking the tones of the local vicar, announced 'Who holdeth our soul in life; and suffereth not our feet to slip.'

The hotel doorman put his fingers in his mouth and gave an ear-splitting whistle.

'Taxi!' he bawled. 'Taxi!'

The coloured boy went up to him on all fours.

'You wanna taxi, man?'

Only the old-time pug seemed to have changed his routine. Whether as a result of therapy or inclination he was no longer shadow boxing. He was skipping vigorously, counting up to a thousand. Naturally he wasn't permitted a rope, but he must have been quite convinced that he had one, because he suddenly tripped over it and, like the hopscotch player, fell flat on his face.

There had been some departures and some arrivals. Among the latter was a young man wearing dark glasses and walking round and round the room, tapping a white stick.

Mr Bettway was at Raine's elbow again.

'Another case of hallucination. He can see just as well as you or I.'

The coloured boy who had suddenly decided to become a taxi pulled up in front of the man with the white stick and called out 'Honk, honk'.

The Malay started sawing away at his violin. It sounded like a Chinese version of *Greensleeves*.

The coloured boy got tired of being a taxi and reverted to his song about black and white man being happy together. And so it would seem. Everybody was doing his own thing, within bounds.

'You know,' said Mr Bettway. 'I shall be almost sorry to leave here, in a way.'

'Really?'

'Yes, really. Mind you, I shall be meeting some old friends on the outside.'

'I should hope so.'

'Mrs Bromley, for instance.'

'Mrs Bromley?'

'Yes, you know. That nice young lady we both danced with.'

'Oh, Lillian.'

'Yes, Lillian. She's been discharged, you know.'

'Discharged! I didn't think she wanted to leave.'

'Well, you know how it is, Mr Raine.'

'Actually, I don't.'

'You will, in time. One gets fond of the old place. Anyway, Mrs Bromley got converted to Catholicism and she's been discharged. I had a lovely letter from her. She's working as a maid and very happy.'

'I'm glad to hear that she's happy. But why work as a maid? I would have though she was far too intelligent.'

'Anything to get away from that husband of hers, Mr Raine. He's a regular beast, I understand.'

The following morning Lord Fife ordered Raine's release from Horseley West Hospital on the understanding that he remained in the care of his daughter, Jacqueline Mary Anne Raine.

Outside the Royal Courts of Justice in the Strand Raine hugged his daughter.

Photographers appeared out of the paving stones. Raine scowled at them.

Both the hug and the scowl were front-paged in the evening papers, but perhaps the scowl got slightly more prominence.

As the photographers and reporters dispersed, Superintendent Clipstone ambled across.

'Well, Jacqueline,' he said. 'I hope you're going to take good care of him.'

'First of all, I'm going to give him a good lunch. Will you join us, Mr Clipstone?'

'I do feel a bit peckish, not having had breakfast this morning. And there are one or two little points I'd like to clear up.'

'Then come along then.'

'No news of Mrs Raine, I suppose?' Clipstone asked.

'None at all. We're both quite worried.'

'I'm a bit worried myself,' said Clipstone.

Over lunch Clipstone dropped his bombshell. Sir Wallis Hilton's examination of the body had established that when Raine stumbled over it Bundock had been dead for over twenty-four hours.

'That's why I'd like to see Mrs Raine,' he said softly. 'Just to ascertain when she left. Was your mother still in the house when you left, Jacqueline?'

'Yes, she was.'

'And they'd been quarrelling?'

'I wouldn't say quarrelling. As I said in my statement, Bundock was trying to persuade Mummy to go back to him and when she refused he called her the most vile names.'

Clipstone nodded sympathetically. It was a sad business. If only he could have a few words with Mrs Raine. He turned to Raine.

'You cannot be certain that it was Oates you saw leaving the house, Mr Raine?'

'Not absolutely certain, no. But I think it was.'

'I checked with the Great Eastern and it would seem that Mrs Raine did not return to the hotel until after seven o'clock that evening, which was after Bundock had died. I'm not saying that she was in the house at the time he was killed, but if he was alive when Mrs Raine left he surely would have followed her.'

'In other words, Superintendent, you suspect my wife?'

'I didn't say that, Mr Raine.'

Then he added gently, 'I'm not in the box now, you know.'

'I'm sorry,' said Raine. 'What I can't understand is how the body could have been there for twenty-four hours without being noticed? All sorts of people called there.'

'You said yourself, Mr Raine, that when you stumbled over it you thought it was a meths drinker sleeping it off.'

'Yes, that is true.'

'I could have made the same mistake myself. In that part of the world one gets so accustomed to seeing meths drinkers asleep in doorways it is taken for granted. They are not usually moved on unless actually obstructing the highway, or the owner of the premises complains.'

'I never allowed them to sleep at Brushfield Street,' said Jacqueline. 'That was one thing I put my foot down about. I didn't want to wake up one morning and find myself incinerated.'

'But they used to call on you?'

'Oh, yes. On all sorts of pretexts, but they knew I was never there on Thursday nights because I did the rounds at Old Ford and slept there.'

'What about other people? Other social workers?'

'The same applied to them. They knew I was at Old Ford Thursday nights and not back till Friday evening.'

'You didn't lock the front door before you left?'

'Never.'

'I would have thought the meths drinkers would have taken advantage of your absence to shelter inside.'

'They did try it on once or twice but when I found out I made it known that if it ever happened again they'd get no more help from me.'

'And the threat worked?'

'The threat worked. Even if I had been in the habit of locking the outside door I could not have done so on that Thursday because Mummy was still there.'

'And Bundock?'

'And Bundock.'

'So they were alone on the premises. I'm afraid, Mr Raine, I shall just have to put out an appeal to your wife to come forward to help us with our enquiries.'

'Of course. I understand.'

Jacqueline had some shopping to do and left the two men over brandy. She paid the bill.

'See you later, Daddy.'

'See you later, Jacqueline.'

'Goodbye, Mr Clipstone.'

'Goodbye, Jacqueline. Thanks for the lunch.'

'A pleasure.'

'You've got a wonderful daughter there, Mr Raine.'

'Yes, I wish she had a wonderful father.'

'Oh, I don't know. What have you got to reproach yourself about?'

'There must have been something wrong, otherwise she wouldn't have left home.'

'Surely that was because her mother had left?'

'Yes, she was pretty upset, but then so was I.'

'Where will you be staying tonight, Mr Raine?'

'With Jacqueline. She's found a two-room flat in Bloomsbury. I'll give you the address.'

'Thanks. It's just in case of any developments.'

'I'd certainly like to hear if you get news of my wife.'

'I promise you I'll let you know immediately.'

'No news of Oates?'

'Not a dicky bird.'

'The pathologist's findings seem to put him in the clear.'

'Not necessarily. He could have stayed on the premises twenty-four hours after having done Bundock in, although it's not likely, I agree. On the other hand it's quite obvious that robbery was the motive for the murder. We know that Bundock was always loaded, but all we found on him was a pocketful of silver.'

'It is not possible that a meths drinker did it?'

'We would have soon heard if any meths drinker had been around with the kind of money Bundock carried on him.'

'Supposing he got scared after the deed and burnt the money?'

'An expensive way for even a meths drinker to keep himself warm,' said Clipstone, drily. 'But I'm afraid we won't be much wiser until Mrs Raine comes forward.'

'I know you said you did not say that you suspected my wife, but have you been thinking along those lines? I'm sorry if I sound as if I had you in the box.'

Clipstone permitted himself the suggestion of a smile.

'I would be a fool if I did not consider every angle and possible motivation, just as I would be a fool if I ignored the fact that you had a pretty good reason for sticking a knife into Bundock's back. You could have lied about seeing Oates in the vicinity, but I don't think you did.

'Also, your wife could easily have been provoked into doing it, but she wouldn't have robbed him, would she? And it does seem to me, as I say, that robbery was the motive.'

10

SUPERINTENDENT CLIPSTONE WAS wrong. Robbery was not the motive behind the murder of Harry George Bundock. Oates had followed Bundock's Jaguar in a stolen car, had seen him park in Brushfield Street and was about to pull up when a meths drinker lurched off the kerbside and in front of his wheels.

Meths drinkers have got this trick of split-second timing down to a fine art. The anxious motorist gets out of his car to survey the casualty and is relieved to see that he has suffered no serious injury beyond shock and slight bruising. The casualty declines the driver's offer to summon an ambulance, knowing that no ambulance will take him, but he does admit that he is weak from hunger and that this is how he came to fall in front of the car. Usually, the motorist puts his hand in his pocket.

Not so Oates. He was driving a stolen car. He was wanted. He couldn't take the risk of hanging around making anxious enquiries about the health of the man under the wheels. Rascal as Oates was, he knew nothing about the minor rascalities of the meths drinkers, and he had no idea that the man was 'chucking a dummy'.

Oates swore under his breath that it was just his bleeding luck, and hurried away.

Oates brooded over the incident all that evening and most of the following day. Like all psychotics, he was given to brooding over real or imagined grievances, over ill winds that blew no good, over strokes of diabolical luck and the perfidy of liberty-takers who brought good villains into disrepute. Harry George Bundock was one such.

He'd had a golden opportunity to 'make a name for himself'. He could have had Harry Bundock all to himself and some silly git had to go and fall in front of the car he'd nicked.

Oates realised that he'd missed a great opportunity, an opportunity not likely to occur again, because normally Bundock had as many minders as the Victoria and Albert. Something of a very private and a very special nature must have taken Bundock way down East alone.

Normally, Bundock never ventured even as far as Aldgate Pump. It just wasn't his manor.

What Oates found even more perplexing was the scruffy little house into which he had seen Bundock disappear. What could the self-styled King of the Underworld be doing in a drum like that? Why was Flash Harry slumming?

Oates decided to find out. So he revisited Spitalfields the following day. It did not say much for the alertness of the local bogeys that the car he had stolen was still parked in Brushfield Street. Such was Oates's low opinion of all police forces that he would not have been much surprised if the meths drinker had still been under the wheels.

What did surprise him was that Bundock's Jaguar was still parked outside 59b. Could it be that Flash Harry went case-o in a place like this? Oates found it difficult to believe, but what else would explain the protracted overnight stay?

He toed the door open, kept it open with his foot and looked up the stairs. On the landing he could discern a humped figure, immobile, but poised as if to slide face downwards down the stairs. Oates propped the door open and soft-footed it up. As he got nearer to the slumped out figure on the landing the light from the street door revealed the handle of a knife sticking out from the man's back. Kneeling down, Oates found himself staring into Bundock's glassy eyes. He had sense enough not to extract the knife.

'Hullo, Bunny. So you copped it at last, did you? Pity, I was going to do you mesself.'

Oates felt frustrated. Coming all this way for nothing. Twice he'd made the journey and here was Bundock as cold as slaw.

It was apparent to Oates that Bundock must have been lured out here by one of the East End mob. He couldn't understand Bundock making a meet in a place like this on his tod. Ah well, the bigger they are the easier they fall.

Oates was about to pay his last respects to Bundock in a time-honoured fashion when it occurred to him to go through the dead man's pockets. He was in luck. It was true what they said about Bundock. He was loaded. He was a walking bank.

When Oates hurried into the street, kicking the prop away from the front door, he was well padded with wads of I Promise To Pay notes on the Bank of England. To say he was elated would have been an under-statement. Ah, well. Every dog has its day and today was Charlie Oates's.

When the car stalled near St Paul's he decided to leave it there and climbed the steps to the *Sir Christopher Wren*. This called for a celebration.

He had a few drinks there and then proceeded down Ludgate Hill to Fleet Street. He went into the *Kings and Keys*. The place was crowded with compositors, linotypers, machine minders, foundry men. A few reporters, long-haired. The Press.

Flushed with drink, Oates was tempted to go across to the long-haired reporters and ask how much they'd pay for a tip-off on a gang murder in the East End. Who? None other than Flash Harry Bundock.

But why waste his time? He didn't need their money and they'd have double-crossed him anyway. They'd keep him chatting while one of them slipped out to the blower and rang the Yard. There's a geezer in the *Kings and Keys* seems to know more than he should do about a gang killing. Says its Harry Bundock. Next thing, ding-a-ling-ding, squeal of brakes and enter the Heavy Mob. Come on, Charlie Boy. Where you bin? We bin looking for you.

No, he didn't need their gelt.

If insanity is anarchy of the mind, then Oates was as mad as they come.

He was aware of the fact that a warrant was out for him and he was dimly aware of the inevitable fact that sooner or later he must expect to get his collar felt in no genteel fashion. Yet as he sank drink after drink he became more and more convinced that this unhappy event would be indefinitely postponed.

His luck had changed.

He was tempted to play it. Go to the dogs or to a spieler.

Then he had a better idea which tickled him immensely. Charlie flattered himself that he had a good sense of humour. He knew that Sadie Bundock had gone back to whoring and had premises in Shepherd Market.

He was taken with the idea of laying her and paying with Harry's money. He swayed out into Fleet Street and waved at a taxi.

It was some time before he could locate Sadie Bundock's place in Shepherd Market. He pressed the top bell.

It was an answer-phone bell. A husky voice came through the sound-box.

'Who is it? Who d'you want?'

'Sadie.'

'Have you been here before?'

'No, but there's always a first time.'

He tried to keep his voice from slurping.

'Come up. It's the top floor.'

The stairs were steep and there were four flights. He climbed slowly, feeling a stabbing pain in his side.

When he got to the top floor his breath came in stabbing gasps. His chest felt as tight as a drum.

It wasn't Sadie who opened the door, but a prim-looking, though shapely, young woman in short black satin dress and frilly white pinafore. She wore glasses. She wasn't pretty, but she was attractive.

'Madam won't keep you a moment,' she said. 'Would you like to take a seat. I'm Lillian, the maid.'

He was only too glad to take a seat in the tiny hall, alongside an oval table on which there were copies of *The Tatler* and *Illustrated London News*. Just like a dentist's waiting room, only the extractions effected here were rather different.

The maid smiled at him.

'Would you like something more naughty to read?'

He hadn't exactly come here for a read but he said he didn't mind and she produced some magazines which looked as if they had been put out in the rain immediately after they came off the machines. They had titles like *Animal Bizarre* and *The Best of Bestiality*.

Oates thought they were disgusting. After all, there was a limit.

'Would you like a drink while you're waiting?'

'Don't mind if I do,' said Oates.

'Whisky?'

She knew it was whisky because he reeked of it. Perhaps if he had another he'd change his mind. Sadie didn't like drunks. They could be more trouble than they were worth.

She was bending forward as she poured the drink and he looked down her cleavage. She slapped his hand away.

'Naughty!'

'But that's what I'm here for,' he protested.

'With madam, not me.'

'Why not you?'

'You'll have to talk to madam about that.'

A cream-painted door opened and there stood Sadie in black lace brassière and black suspenderbelt, nothing else, hand on her size 42 hips.

'What's he got to talk to me about?'

'He fancies me, madam.'

'Does he? The saucy old sod.'

Oates grinned at her.

'I fancy both of you.'

'Oh, you do, do you. Well come on in.'

Oates got unsteadily to his feet and followed her into the bedroom dimly lit by a pink-shaded lamp.

Lillian came in with them. Sadie gave him a look of cold appraisal. He was as white as a sheet.

'You feel all right?'

'Sure, I'm okay.'

'Well, have you got a nice present for two naughty girls?'

He waved an arm.

'How much you like?'

'If you want two of us it's a score.'

'A score! That's a bit steep isn't?'

'Listen, love,' said Sadie patiently. 'If you can't afford my price you shouldn't come to Mayfair. Try one of them Paddington scrubbers.'

'I didn't say I couldn't afford your price. I said the stairs was a bit steep, that's all. 'Course I can afford a score. Fifty, if you like.'

What did it matter? It was her ex-old man's money anyway. That was the funny part about it. Dead funny, it was.

'Oh, well. That's different,' she said. 'Make it fifty and we'll give you a real nice time.'

Both Sadie and Lillian stared as he pulled a wad of notes out of his pocket and began to count out ten fivers. He looked a right mug. Notes fluttered around his feet like leaves falling off a tree.

Eventually Sadie counted the fifty out herself in front of him just to demonstrate that he wasn't being cheated. Then she picked up the fallen notes and stuffed them into his pockets.

'You robbed a bank or something?'

He laughed.

'You'd be surprised.'

Wouldn't she, eh! Not half she wouldn't. Life did have its compensations after all.

Lillian was pulling the black satin number over her head and Sadie was putting the ten fivers into a vase containing dried flowers.

'Makes 'em grow better,' she giggled, looking at him over a shoulder the size of a York ham.

He was sitting on the bed, holding his side.

'What's the matter, love. Aren't you feeling well?'

'I'm all right,' he said. 'It must have been them stairs.'

Sadie went and sat beside him on the bed. The springs creaked.

'Listen, love. Are you sure you're up to it? I mean to say if you can't climb a few stairs you're not up to the other are you? Wouldn't you like to come back some other time?'

'No, I wouldn't like to come back some other time.'

He felt that his virility was being impugned. He would have them both if it killed him. He'd show them. They were not going to cast doubts on Charlie Oates's masculinity. His forehead was glistening. He fumbled with the knot of his tie.

'Let me unbutton your collar,' said Lillian.

'I'll unbutton his flies.'

'It's a zip, anyway,' he said.

'That makes it all the easier, doesn't it. My, what's this little thing here? That's no use to two big girls, is it?'

Lillian was taking off his shoes.

'One, two, unbuckle his shoes. I say, where d'you get these socks? They look like hospital socks to me.'

She tugged at his trousers.

'Lift your bottom,' she said. 'Turn over.'

He did. The trousers slithered down his legs. Meticulously, she folded them and draped them over a hanger. As she did so another wad of notes fell out of the rear hip pocket.

Sadie picked it up.

'I'll just take our present, shall I, love?'

He nodded.

'Sure, take what you want.'

'You did say fifty, love, didn't you?'

'That's right. Is that enough?'

'Bless you, love. You're very generous. Thirty-five, forty, forty-five, fifty. That's right, isn't it, love? I'm putting the rest back in your pocket.'

She'd be grinning on the other side of her face, he reckoned, if she knew where it came from. She was just another liberty-taker like her ex-old man. Did she think he was so pissed he didn't know she had taken a century off him? Then just let her wait until he'd had his fun, then he'd give both of 'em a right hander and take the hundred back and any more that happened to be in the flower vase, come to that, just as a bonus. Teach them to take liberties with Charlie Oates. He wasn't born yesterday.

They were both on the bed with him now, both nude, except that Lillian kept her glasses on. She had one hand around his scrotum, the other encouraging his stamen. Then, expertly, she slipped a sheath over him.

'We don't want any little babies, do we?' she cooed. 'Gosh.'

Suddenly, he was on top of one of them. He would never know which because, in the moment of ecstasy, he blacked out.

'He's passed out,' said Lillian.

Sadie pulled his head up by the simple expedient of tugging at his hair. She looked at his face and knew the worst. It was every prostitute's nightmare and it had happened once before in her life. Twice was too much.

'Passed out, my arse. He's dead.'

Lillian screamed. Screamed loud enough to be heard at Hyde Park Corner.

'Get him off me then, he weighs a ton. Gosh.'

Sadie gave Oates a shove and he rolled over on to the floor. The thud shook the bedside lamp. He had proved himself.

'What are we going to do?' Lillian wailed. 'Ring the police?'

'Are you mad? Do you think I want the Law round here?'

'Do you think I do? I can't afford to be mixed up in a scandal. Gosh, if my husband finds out.'

'Your husband doesn't mind taking the money, does he?' said Sadie angrily. 'Give me that 'phone. I'll call Harry. He'll know how to get rid of this stiff.'

She dialled Harry George Bundock's number. Not surprisingly, there was no reply

Lillian was kneeling at the bedside. It was Sadie's turn to scream.

'What you doing?'

'Praying,' said Lillian, then began softly, *'Hail Mary, full of grace....'*

'Oh, get up off your knees,' Sadie shouted. 'Do something! Ring that ponce husband of yours.'

'I can't,' Lillian snivelled. 'He thinks I'm at the pictures.'

II

BOTH RAINE AND his daughter gave evidence at the inquest on Harry George Bundock. They followed Sadie Bundock, who merely gave formal evidence of having identified the body.

Jacqueline was called first. She stated that on the day previous to the discovery of the body by her father she had seen her mother at 59b Brushfield Street, E.1. Her mother was very upset and tried to persuade her to give up the work in the East End. She told her mother that she would think it over. While they were talking Bundock arrived. Yes, her mother had been living with Bundock. Yes, she had left him.

Bundock tried to persuade her mother to return to him. When she refused he became abusive and called her obscene names. She could not bear hearing her mother reviled and so she left. Yes, she now knew that it had been a mistake to leave. She spent the night at Old Ford and did not return until the following evening. Yes, she did see her father on the premises. He was at the top of the stairs and holding a bread knife wrapped in a tissue. Yes, they went to the police station together. No, she had no idea of her mother's present address.

'Thank you, Miss Raine,' said the Coroner.

As Jacqueline stepped out of the box Raine stepped into it. He gave her hand a squeeze in passing.

Yes, his name was Roland John Raine. Yes, he was a barrister. Yes, he was on the roll of Queen's Counsel. No, he was no longer practising. At least, he had not been practising recently. How long? Possibly two or three years. He could not be more exact? Yes, he could. Just over two years. Was that for health reasons? Partly, yes.

He had been in hospital? Yes, he had been in hospital. Which hospital? To be explicit, two. Brinstead Manor for twenty-four hours and Horseley West Hospital for about two weeks. Were these specialist hospitals?

'Surely,' Raine replied, 'as a coroner you should know that they are both mental hospitals? If you are trying to drag it out of me you have succeeded.'

The Coroner assured Raine that nobody was trying to drag anything out of anybody. They were here today to enquire into the circumstances surrounding the death of a Mr Harry George Bundock. Was he in care of West Horseley Hospital on the day that Bundock died?

No, he was not. Had he been discharged from Horseley West Hospital? No, he had not. Had he been a voluntary patient? No, he had been committed there for observation. Then he had left without permission? Yes, he had left without permission.

He'd run away? If the Coroner wished to put it that way, yes—he'd run away. Why?

'Because I didn't like it there,' said Raine. 'No sane person would like it there.'

This brought a snigger of laughter into the tiny courtroom not far from what had been Poplar Town Hall where old George Lansbury had harangued the cause of Peace.

'If there is any more laughter I will clear the Court,' said the Coroner. 'This is not a laughing matter.'

He then proceeded to ask Raine where he was on the day that Harry George Bundock was killed. Raine said he would like to write the address down as it so happened he was staying with a lady.

Grudgingly, the Coroner complied with the request, although he wasn't sure he approved of these displays of gallantry.

Raine wrote the address down and handed it to the clerk, who handed it to the Coroner, who asked Superintendent Gretton of the Murder Squad if he would like to have it. The Yard man said he knew the address. It was in Mr Raine's statement.

If Raine had been representing a client he would have protested that the Coroner was behaving as if the witness was not so much a witness as a defendant.

Why did he go to 59b Brushfield Street? Because he had been told his wife was there. And was she? No. Who was there? There was no living person. Was there a dead person? Yes. Who?

'You know perfectly well who it was,' said Raine. 'Bundock.'

The Coroner replied that he did not know. He had to take Raine's word for it. Where was Bundock's body? At the top of the stairs. He stumbled over it. He'd stumbled over it and yet not realised it was a body? Not at first. He thought it was a meths drinker asleep. When did he realise that it was the body of Bundock? When he'd opened the door of his daughter's room and seen it in the light at close quarters.

He knew Bundock? Yes, he knew Bundock. In what capacity? He had defended him at the Central Criminal Courts. The Old Bailey? Yes, the Old Bailey. And he had obtained a verdict of Not Guilty? Yes.

'In other words, Mr Raine, you got him off?'

'I did not say that. The jury returned a verdict of Not Guilty.'

'Don't let's split hairs, Mr Raine. Would you not agree that it was in no small measure due to your skill as defending counsel that Bundock was acquitted?'

'That is not for me to say.'

'One would have thought that Bundock would have been grateful to you?'

'At the Criminal Bar one does not expect gratitude. Sometimes one is lucky to get the fee.'

Again there was laughter and the Coroner frowned as if tempted to implement his threat, but continued with the questioning.

'Mr Raine, you must have felt very embittered when your wife ran off with Bundock?'

'Embittered is an understatement.'

'Thank you, Mr Raine. That will be all.'

Raine stepped down, feeling that he had not done too well. A man with his experience should not have allowed himself to be goaded.

Jacqueline clutched his hand.

'Who does that man think he is?' she whispered.

'Counsel for the prosecution,' Raine answered in a voice deliberately loud enough to be heard all over the court.

The Coroner returned a verdict of murder against some person or persons unknown.

Outside the court, newspaper and television reporters and photographers converged on Raine. No, he told a television man, he was not prepared to take part in a studio programme called 'The World of Crime'. No, he told the others, he had no idea who might have killed Bundock. A man like Bundock would have lots of enemies.

'Your guess is as good as mine,' said Raine. 'And I'm not attempting to guess.'

'You have no idea where your wife is at the moment, Mr Raine?'

'You are the newspaper reporters. If you can trace her please let me know.'

'You would go to her?'

'But of course.'

'Why do you suppose she did not answer the appeal to come forward to help the police with their enquiries, Mr Raine?'

'Probably because she doesn't want to be pestered by chaps like you,' Raine replied, irritably.

Nobody asked about Charlie Oates. Nobody knew that Charlie Oates was not only dead but had been buried 'on the rates'.

One way and another Sadie had had quite a time of it. Eventually, she just had to ring Savile Row and tell them that a client had died in her bed.

No, she had no idea who he was and there were no papers of identification on the body. There wasn't even any money.

Oates was kept on ice for a few days while perfunctory enquiries were made and then buried by the Westminster City Council. Nobody bothered to take the dead man's fingerprints and the death of an unknown man on the bed of a Shepherd Market whore didn't even make the newspapers.

Then, on top of it, she'd had to take a taxi all the way to the East End to identify Harry. It was enough to drive a poor woman potty. Then she'd gone to Kenyon's to make the funeral arrangements, telling them to spare no expense. After which she ordered her own floral tribute in the form of a broken pillar. She wanted it made of forget-me-nots but was told they were out of season.

On the evening of the inquest on Bundock the chief of the Yard Murder Squad called round to see Raine. Tom Gretton was a younger man than Clipstone, but quite friendly.

'Sorry to drop in on you like this out of the blue,' he said.

'Not at all,' said Raine. 'Can I offer you a drink?'

'I've had a hard day. I wouldn't say no to a small vodka, if you have one.'

'Jacqueline!' Raine called. 'Have we any vodka?'

'Yes, Daddy. I got a bottle at Oddbins today.'

'We have to watch the pennies,' Raine explained.

'Don't we all?'

'I think I'll have a whisky, darling,' said Raine.

Jacqueline poured the drinks and left the men, busying herself in the kitchen.

'Cheers,' said Raine.

'Good health, sir.'

The Yard man appeared to be studying his drink.

'I thought that Coroner was throwing his weight about a bit this morning.'

'I thought so, too,' said Raine. 'But you must know what some of these Coroners are like, Superintendent. If the case attracts a few reporters they like to show off, hoping to get quoted in the papers.'

'You're right. There's one thing that worries me.'

'Yes, what's that?'

'This woman—what's her name, Prepend?'

'That's right. What about her?'

'We've been trying to get confirmation from her that you stayed with her on the day Bundock was murdered, but either she's gone away or she isn't answering the door. She certainly isn't answering the 'phone.'

'She did tell me that she'd been subjected to obscene calls. Also, I remember that when I was in the house there the 'phone rang several times and she wouldn't answer it. And when a police car arrived outside she would not answer the front door bell.'

'You do appreciate, Mr Raine, that I have to get confirmation from her that you were with her on the evening of the 27th of last month and that you had been with her since early that morning?'

'I do appreciate it.'

'I'm thinking of calling on her again this evening. Would you mind coming round with me, Mr Raine?'

'Not in the least. Glad to be of any assistance. Another drink?'

'No, thanks. That was fine. Let's go, shall we?'

'Yes, let's do that.'

Raine called out to Jacqueline, 'Won't be long, darling. I'm just popping out with Mr Gretton.'

Jacqueline came to the kitchen door, eyed both men with just a flicker of concern in those limpid green eyes.

'Okay, Daddy. I'm making a casserole.'

'It smells delicious.'

'Goodnight, Mr Gretton.'

'Goodnight, Miss Raine.'

Outside, Raine got into the police car with Gretton.

'Chester Square Mews South,' Gretton told the driver. 'Stop on the corner. We don't want to frighten the good lady.'

Raine's mouth puckered at Gretton's description of Eileen Prepend. He had no means of knowing whether it was intended to be ironic or not.

'A nice evening,' said the Yard man.

'Yes, very.'

Ten minutes later the car pulled up at one end of Chester Square Mews South.

'We're in luck,' said Gretton as they walked down the cobbled mews. 'There's a light on.'

He rang the bell. Raine recognised the chimes sounding within. Gretton had to ring the bell again. It was some minutes before Eileen Prepend opened the door. She was wearing a godetia patterned house-coat and smoking a cigarette which had obviously only just been lit.

Gretton raised his hat.

'Good evening. Are you Mrs Prepend?'

'That's me. Why?'

'I'm Superintendent Gretton of New Scotland Yard, but don't let that alarm you. This is just a formal enquiry. May we come in for a minute?'

Eileen Prepend took the cigarette out of her mouth.

'No, I'm sorry. It's not convenient. I've got company. You'll have to come back some other time.'

I've got company. The pro's age-old euphemism for 'I've got a client'.

The Yard remained pleasant, but there was just the slightest edge to his voice as he replied, 'In that case we will have to talk on the doorstep, won't we?'

'What is all this about?' she asked, flicking ash.

She had scarcely looked at Raine.

'You know Mr Raine here?'

Eileen Prepend now turned a pair of scrutinising eyes on Raine. She shook her head.

'Should I?'

'I just want to confirm that Mr Raine spent the night of the twenty-seventh of last month under your roof, Mrs Prepend. That is all.'

'He certainly did not.'

Gretton looked at Raine now.

'I certainly did,' said Raine. 'Why, I could describe the furnishings of the house.'

Eileen flicked more ash. Her eyes narrowed.

'I might be able to describe the inside of Buckingham Palace,' she said. 'But that wouldn't make me Queen of England.'

'That is an irrelevancy, madam, if you don't mind my saying so,' said Gretton. 'Are you saying that you don't know Mr Raine here?'

'I only saw him once before in my life when he tried to thumb a lift from me at Epsom. I didn't like the look of him. So I drove on.'

'You are quite certain about that, Mrs Prepend?'

'As God's my judge.'

'Thank you, Mrs Prepend. Goodnight.'

Gretton raised his hat again. As Eileen Prepend was closing the door Raine noticed a man's hat on the hallstand. It was a velour with a little feather in the band. The man who had no time to go to concerts.

'Well, that's that,' said Gretton as they walked back along the mews.

'Yes, that's that.'

'I'm afraid I shall have to charge you, Mr Raine.'

'Yes, I suppose you will.'

He felt numb.

'After you,' said Gretton, opening the door of the car.

'Thanks.'

Gretton got in after him. He leaned towards the driver

'Drop Mr Raine back at his home first, will you, Blake.'

'Yes, sir.'

'I thought you were going to charge me?' said Raine.

'I'm charging you to try to forget the nightmare, Mr Raine. That woman was lying her head off.'

'I know she was,' said Raine. 'But how do you know?'

'Because I'd already checked with the neighbours and they told me they'd seen you leaving her house on the morning of the twenty-eighth. Sometimes it's a good thing neighbours are so inquisitive, isn't it?'

'Sometimes, yes,' said Raine. 'Well, I must say, that's a great relief.'

A few minutes later the police car stopped. The driver got out to open the door for Raine. Raine gripped Gretton's hand.

'Thanks,' he said.

'Don't mention it. Enjoy the casserole.'

'I will.'

'Oh, by the way.'

'Yes?'

'If you get news of your wife you'll let us know?'

'Of course. Goodnight.'

'Goodnight.'

The car rolled away, and with it, Raine hoped, the nightmare.

Jacqueline opened the door and he could see that her eyes were wet. She clung to him.

'Daddy! I was afraid that you might not be coming back.'

'So was I—for a minute or two,' he said.

Jacqueline had bought a bottle of Gevry-Chambertin to go with the casserole and they clinked glasses. Yes, perhaps the nightmare was ending at last.

'If only Mummy was here,' he said.

Jacqueline suddenly got up from the table and ran from the room, sobbing.

'Jacqueline! Jacqueline!'

He followed her to her room. He could hear her sobbing. He knocked at the door.

'Jacqueline, can I come in?'

'No, Daddy, please. I'd rather you didn't.'

'Why not? What's wrong? I know you're upset about Mummy, but so am I. She'll turn up one fine day, believe me.'

'No, Daddy, she won't. She's gone away for good.'

'How do you know. Look Jacqueline, I can't talk to you through the door. Come and finish the dinner you cooked. It's delicious.'

'No, I don't want to.'

'Oh, come on, Jacqueline. Don't be a baby.'

Then she was suddenly howling like a baby. Raine flung the door open and went in. She was face downwards on the bed.

He sat on the side of the bed and put his arms round her.

'Hush, darling,' he tried to coax her. 'Hush. Things are never as bad as they seem.'

She turned around to face him, those big green eyes of hers awash with tears, and put both arms around his neck so fiercely that he found it difficult to breath.

'Yes, they are,' she sobbed. 'They're worse.'

'Worse than what, darling?'

'Worse than what you think.'

'Darling, the worst is over.'

'No it isn't. The worst is yet to come.'

'What do you mean, my pet? Tell me.'

'I know why Mummy's gone away.'

'Why, darling?'

'Because....'

'Because of what?'

'Because she doesn't want to have to give evidence against me.'

'Jacqueline, what on earth are you talking about?'

As he asked the question the look in her eyes supplied the answer. No, the nightmare wasn't over.

Quite often in his career Raine had heard an accused person in the box say 'I don't know what came over me.' Invariably he had replied, 'I suggest to you that you knew perfectly well what you were doing.'

He had never anticipated that he would ever hear his daughter echo those words, so often heard in the criminal courts. *I don't know what came over me.*

'I was cutting sandwiches, Daddy, trying not to listen to all the vile names he was calling Mummy.'

Suddenly she had gone very calm as if describing something that had happened in a dream, something that had not actually happened to her at all.

'It didn't seem to matter to him that I was in the same room and that he was talking to—raving at, I should say—my mother. I'd never heard such language even from the meths drinkers.

'Mummy kept saying "Please, not in front of my daughter", but it made no difference to him. He just went raving on and on like a man possessed, getting filthier and filthier all the time.

'At one point I put the bread knife down and clapped my hands to my ears. "For God's sake," I implored him, "stop it, will you? I cannot stand any more." He paid no attention and went on and on with his foul abuse. I picked up the bread knife and then I don't know what came over me. I saw the knife sticking out from between his shoulders.

'Mummy screamed and ran out. He tried to follow her, but collapsed on the landing. I ran down the stairs, calling out to Mummy but by the time I got into the street she'd disappeared.

'I didn't go to Old Ford that night. I just walked the streets for hours and hours and hours, having no idea of time or place or anything.

'What guided my steps back to Brushfield Street I don't know. Instinct, perhaps. And there you were—standing at the top of the stairs.

'That's the whole story, Daddy.'

'Oh, my darling.'

He folded her in his arms and he saw his own tears splash on her caramel-coloured hair.

'And that's why Mummy won't be coming back,' she said.

'Oh, yes she will, my pet,' he whispered. 'Oh, yes she will. And we'll all be together again. Leave this to me. I'll see you through.'

He got up and went into his own room to use the telephone. The nightmare was by no means over, but this was the sort of challenge he needed. When he got through he asked to speak to Superintendent Gretton.

'Could you come back here, Mr Gretton?' he asked. 'I have something of importance to tell you. No, it's not about my wife. It's about my daughter.'

12

A SURGEON DOES not usually operate on members of his own family. Neither does a barrister represent his kith and kin in court. Even so, it was not without some misgiving that Raine learned that counsel briefed for the defence of Jacqueline was none other than Reggie Paignton, Q.C. Raine could not think of a worse choice.

Raine had always thought that Reggie would have made a better actor than barrister, the 'Who's For Tennis?' type coming through french windows, brass-buttoned blazer over white flannels and co-respondent shoes, a profile something between the late Owen Nares and Ivor Novello.

Reggie Paignton was bland, effusive and utterly shallow. His knowledge of Law was sketchy, but he was well-meaning and had an air of ingratiating sincerity as well as immense charm. He had hosts of friends. Everybody liked Reggie. The secret of his success was sheer mediocrity.

As far as Raine could see the obvious plea for Jacqueline was Not Guilty to murder and Not Guilty to manslaughter. Reggie couldn't see this. He thought it should be Not Guilty to murder but Guilty to manslaughter. He always played safe, did Reggie.

He argued that it would be quite obvious to judge and jury that Jacqueline had plunged the knife into Bundock's back, albeit under extreme provocation. On her own admission she had picked up the knife and then—'I don't know what came over me.' One could not expect to convince the jury that Bundock had fallen backwards on to a bread knife, could one? Plead guilty to manslaughter. The judge would award a twelve months' suspended sentence and Jacqueline would walk out of court a free woman. It was as simple as that. After all, the sympathy of both judge and jury would be with Jacqueline.

Better by far for her to admit that she had stabbed Bundock than pretend that it was an accident. Honesty pays, even at the Bar, Reggie claimed. Never underestimate the intelligence of the jury. Never exasperate the judge.

'Leave it to me, Roland,' he said. 'There's a good chap.'

It was all very well, but supposing Jacqueline came up against one of those judges who are forever deploring violence in the young and deploring the leniency shown by their brother judges? Raine could hear him drooling words of modulated sympathy for a young lady suffering the agony of hearing her mother so vilely traduced. Nevertheless, sympathy must be tempered with justice. It was no trivial act to plunge a knife into any man's back, even allowing for mitigating circumstances, even granted that the man was a beast—even the most bestial of men have a right to the same protection in law as the most worthy citizen.

'Bearing in mind all the circumstances of this tragic case,' Raine could hear this imaginary judge intoning, 'I would be failing in my duty if I did not sentence the accused to two years' imprisonment. But for her youth and previous excellent character the sentence would have been far heavier.'

One of the happier aspects of the tragedy was that, as soon as the news broke of Jacqueline's impending trial, Veronica came out of hiding. In her confused and shattered state of mind she had thought that her disappearance would have the effect of throwing suspicion upon herself rather than on her daughter. She had been staying with a friend in one of the more remote Orkney islands.

She moved in with Raine, occupying what had been Jacqueline's room. Although Raine was overjoyed to see her again, reunited as they were in acute unhappiness, he did not find that she gave him strength. She was forever blaming herself for what had happened. However true that might have been, her constantly expressed remorse did not help matters.

As the day of the trial got nearer so Veronica got increasingly agitated. So much so that Raine began to fear that she was due for a nervous breakdown. He begged her to try to relax and stop pacing up and down, forever repeating that it was all her fault.

What has happened has happened, he told her time and time

again, nor all our tears shall rub out a word of it. It was no use indulging in orgies of self-recrimination.

They came close to quarrelling violently. How could he be so apparently unperturbed about the situation of his own daughter due to appear at the Old Bailey on a manslaughter charge? In the past, on the eve of a trial, she had seen him far more tensed up over the fate of a client, a stranger.

He tried to explain to her that his outward calm, even composure, was something he had forced upon himself for Jacqueline's sake. They owed it to her to put on the bravest possible front during her ordeal. The worst part about it was the waiting, the suspense. He would be glad when the day of the trial came round, because in spite of certain misgivings regarding Reggie Paignton's conduct of the defence the end of the day would see Jacqueline restored to them.

'Please believe that, Veronica,' he said. 'Because if you lose faith I shall lose faith and Jacqueline will be lost to us and she is all we have.'

'Oh, for God's sake, Roland,' she cried. 'I think I'd admire you more if you'd socked me for being such a bitch to you.'

'Darling,' he said. 'Haven't we had enough of violence?'

She suddenly began to cry and he lost patience with her.

'My little baby girl in Holloway awaiting trial,' she whimpered. 'I can't bear the thought of it.'

'Now, come off it, Veronica,' he said. 'Your little baby girl has for the last three years been working among one of the most debased and degraded sections of the human race, meths drinkers. So believe me, she isn't exactly crushed by the experience of Holloway. She's a tough baby is your little baby girl, make no mistake about it.'

Veronica dabbed at her eyes.

'I'm sorry,' she said. 'I only wish I could change places with her, that's all.'

'There you go again,' he said. 'Self-recrimination. Oh, to hell with it. Let's have a drink.'

'Yes, let's have a drink.'

'You know something,' he said. 'On that day I walked to Brushfield Street I was so weak I sat down on the steps of St Paul's and you know what I was reminded of?'

'I know,' she said. 'It was just before we got married and we heard Verdi's *Requiem* there, sitting together, hand in hand. I was just about Jacqueline's age then and I felt our love was just like those glorious voices we were listening to. Did you feel that, darling?'

'I did,' he said. 'I did. And I believe it was.'

'Do you mean that, Roland?'

'Of course I do.'

'Thank you. I'll fix that drink.'

'Did you know that Jacqueline's a marvellous cook?'

'Of course she is. I taught her, didn't I?'

'Sorry, so you did.'

'When all this is over,' said Veronica, coming back with the drinks. 'It would be nice to go away somewhere, just the three of us.'

'Yes, let's do that.'

'Where shall we go?'

'I think we'll leave the choice to Jacqueline.'

'Good idea.'

'So long as she doesn't decide on taking us through a leper colony for our sins.'

'I think that's a phase in her life that's over for the time being.'

'Let's hope so.'

'God bless you, my darling.'

'God bless.'

'And cheers, Jacqueline.'

'Yes. Cheers, Jacqueline. Keep your pecker up, old girl.'

'You're going to see her tomorrow?'

'Yes, how was she today?'

'Complaining that she was putting on weight.'

'You know, if it were tulip time we could have taken Jacqueline to Holland.'

'I think it might bore her, drifting down those canals.'

'Perhaps so. I must confess it bored me once the novelty was over.'

'Now I'll tell you something. I was bored too.'

'But we weren't bored with each other.'

'No, I don't think we were.'

'Do you think we will ever be bored with each other?'

'I don't think so.'

The telephone pip-pipped. Raine went to answer it.

'Who was it?' Veronica asked when he came back.

'Reggie Paignton. He says the hearing has been brought forward to Monday.'

'Thank God. The sooner the better. How did Reggie sound?'

'Oh, you know Reggie. Always on top of the world. Nothing to worry about, old chap. Everything in the garden's lovely.'

'Remember that ghastly dinner we once had at their place?'

'I do indeed. Potted shrimps or grapefruit segments, tomato soup, plaice and chips, tinned fruit salad, instant coffee and Murray Mints.'

'You've forgotten the wine.'

'I have not. It was elderberry.'

'By the way, we never asked them back, did we?'

'No, and I have news for you. We're invited for dinner the day of the hearing. The three of us.'

'Oh, my God, no. I think Jacqueline would prefer to stay in Holloway than eat at their place.'

'We have an easy get out. You ring up and say it occurs to you that we owe them a dinner—you can bet they keep a check—and invite them here.'

'Oh, hell, must I?'

'No, but it would be better than going there. After all, we ought to make a gesture. Reggie's made a grand gesture. He says he won't accept a fee for defending Jacqueline.'

'Oh, what an excruciating bastard he is!'

'Yes, he is, isn't he?'

'Now that we're talking about the Paigntons, shall I tell you something?'

'Please do.'

'It was because of the Paigntons that I first began to think of leaving you. I thought if they are his great friends, well I just didn't want to know. I'd look for somebody who had a different set of values. Instead I found myself with somebody who had no values at all. The reason I did it, I think was because he was the very antithesis of everything the Paigntons of this world stand for.'

'Was that a good and sufficient reason.'

'Quite frankly, Roland, my love, no. And I freely admit it.'

'Well, don't let's go into all that again. What are we going to do when Jacqueline comes out?'

'Let's leave it to Jacqueline, shall we?'

'Yes, let's do that.'

'One thing is for sure, we don't go to the Paigntons for dinner.'

'Then they come here?'

'I think we'll leave the decision to Jacqueline.'

'You know what Jacqueline told me the other week? She said we gave her too much love and she was afraid of becoming a spoiled brat.'

'As if she ever could.'

'That's what I said.'

'On the other hand I can see what she was getting at. She's very much like me, darling, and she wanted to see another side of the coin of life.'

'Well, you've both seen it now. I suppose I have too, briefly. Perhaps there was a great deal of wisdom in what Jacqueline meant—there is a danger of us all becoming spoiled brats in our middle class smugness—and I did not realise it until recently.'

'Now who's indulging in self-recrimination?'

'I'm not really. I'm trying to widen my sights on life, to try to be more understanding, more tolerant of the weak, but less tolerant of those who presume to tell us what we should do and what we should not do.'

'Them's rash words coming from a man of law.'

'I wonder. The things I've seen recently make me wonder if the lawyers really know what it's all about.'

'Do they really care so long as they make a fat living out of it? Do you think Reggie Paignton would lose a minute's sleep if Jacqueline got three years on Monday?'

'Veronica! For God's sake, don't talk like that.'

'I'm sorry,' she said. 'But I can't help giving voice to my worst fears.'

13

ONE OF THE women's wards at Horseley West Hospital was called 'Mimosa'. There was no particular reason why it should have been called 'Mimosa' any more than that the next hut should have been named 'Jonquil' or the hut on the other side 'Iris'. It was felt that it helped to give patients a sense of identity in the same way that people in suburbia gave incongruous names like *Mon Repos* and *Shangrila* to quite characterless houses.

Dr Eric Glazer was all in favour of encouraging patients to identify themselves with themselves, to give them a sense of belonging as opposed to the bleak feeling of having been rejected by society. It was all very much a sham device which did not even deceive the patients. For every woman in the 'Mimosa' ward knew that officially it was the ward for chronics.

Dr Glazer was against the facile system of putting all mentally disturbed cases into rigid categories, as so many of his colleagues did, and then giving the patients in each category identical treatment—analysis, drugs and shock treatment.

He was of the opinion that it just was not possible to have hard and fast rules about what was normal and what was abnormal in human behaviour. It is possible to say that one person is tall and another is short, one is fat and one is thin, providing that a physical average has been agreed upon.

It was just not possible to draw these same sharp distinctions between what is mentally sick and what is mentally healthy. It could be argued that any behaviour prohibited by law was the behaviour of a mentally sick person. By the same token, it could be argued that any individual behaving in a manner likely to give offence to his fellow men (and women) should receive the label of 'abnormal'.

On the other hand, as often as not, particularly in cases where a patient had been committed to hospital at the request of his or her family, he had found that it was the family itself which was really in need of treatment and that the committed person was the victim of abnormal relatives. Sometimes he found the thought quite terrifying and for that reason he was in favour of subjecting the relatives to analysis at the same time as the patient. Unfortunately, it was not always possible, but whenever he had succeeded in getting a family to submit to group analysis he had formed the opinion that the patient should be discharged and the hospitalisation reversed.

Perhaps Dr Glazer was not an orthodox psychiatrist. Not all his theories would have found favour among his colleagues. For instance, he believed in and practised sexual relationships between therapist and patient, behaviour that would have got a general practitioner struck off for gross professional misconduct.

Yet Dr Glazer had no qualms about it. Sexual associations between male psychotherapist and female patient were as common as those between employer and private secretary, between bachelor householder and lady housekeeper. He saw nothing reprehensible in it as it helped to establish that confidence between patient and doctor which can only be attained through the most intimate of physical relationships.

Freud's disciples had indulged in this form of therapy, and in America it was common knowledge that the psychiatrist's couch had usurped the enviable reputation of that once enjoyed by the Hollywood casting director's.

It was argued that sexual realisation between therapist and patient helps communication and that, putting it crudely, the lowering of intimate garments was followed by the lowering of mental barriers. The physical means justified the psychiatric ends.

Dr Glazer's very personal form of therapy was a constant topic among the chronics in the 'Mimosa' ward and was accepted as part of the Horseley West way of life.

Those who hadn't made it with Dr Glazer, or 'responded to treatment' as it was laughingly referred to, had no social standing in 'Mimosa'. Those who had made no secret of it and some of those who hadn't even pretended that they had. It was the subject of much bawdy and vulgar discussion, giving rise to various jests about double glazing.

One remarkable aspect of Dr Glazer's so personal form of therapy was that his nurse, Lois Summerton, was always present, although she usually made a pretence of looking out of the window when the patient started to respond.

Nobody could agree on whether Lois Summerton was Glazer's mistress or not. Christine Thirkell, a kleptomaniac who had been at Horseley West for eighteen months, maintained she wasn't.

'I mean t'say,' Christine would point out, 'how could he possibly cope? I don't care how many sex drive pills he prescribed for himself—and I've seen him take them by the handful—he just couldn't cope with her as well as us, could he now? It stands to reason, doesn't it?'

'His prick stands for no reason at all, darling,' drawled Judy Prince, an arsonist.

'Really, Judy. I don't think that's very flattering,' Christine replied.

Judy Prince was an actress long past playing *ingénue* roles. For many years she had been the mistress of a rich impresario and when he dropped her for another and younger lady of the theatre she had gone round the countryside burning down any theatre so ill-advised as to stage one of his productions.

For a long time it was suspected that the impresario himself was responsible for the conflagrations in order to get the insurance money. It took years of patient investigation by fire assessors as well as police to establish that Judy Prince was the culprit. The prosecution was not very pleased when the judge passed a suspended sentence on Judy on the understanding that she went into hospital for psychiatric treatment.

'Oh, don't take it personally,' Judy replied. 'I wouldn't touch Glazer with a barge pole.'

'What you mean is, Judy, he won't touch you with his,' Christine retorted.

'Christine, darling, must you be so unbearably coarse?'

'You know you're only jealous because you're not getting it.'

'Darling, I've had more of it than you've had hot dinners.'

'Now who's being coarse?'

'I must say it's a bit off-putting at first,' said Molly Brereton, who had poisoned her husband with weed killer.

At her trial she had caused unseemly laughter in court by her reply to a question by prosecuting Counsel, 'Why did you administer weed killer to your husband, Mrs Brereton?'

'Because he was a weed.'

Perhaps it was this reply and a number of others equally frivolous that earned her hospitalisation instead of imprisonment.

'What's off-putting at first?' Christine asked.

'Having Lois Summerton in the same room. I don't like doing it in front of other people. It's not nice.'

'He *has* to have Lois there. Don't you see if one of us created trouble about it, wrote to the Ministry or something, he'd be able to say that the charge nurse was always present at therapy sessions. Then they'd ask Nurse Summerton if she'd seen anything improper take place and she'd say No, never. Who do you think they'd believe? You—or Nurse Summerton?'

An endless subject of discussion was the various methods of approach made by Dr Glazer. Sometimes he would sit alongside the patient, take her hand and use it to stroke himself. On other occasions he would sit in front of her so that their knees were touching and then gently he would say, 'Open your knees, close them. Open, close, open, close.' This would go on for as long as five minutes after which the woman would either be ready to submit or to run out screaming. If she attempted the latter she would be put under heavy sedation and if she complained that Dr Glazer had attempted to seduce her it would be put down to hallucinations. Electric shock treatment might be recommended.

Christine turned to a newcomer to 'Mimosa', a girl not yet twenty. She had arrived at the hospital in a state of catatonic stupor, the state in which the patient has withdrawn from all human contact, almost as if sleepwalking, as if the entire nervous system is in abeyance and refuses to be aroused. Physiological checks, however, reveal that contrary to all outward appearances the patient is intensely alert and hypersensitive to everything going on around her.

'What about you, sweetie?' Christine asked. 'Has Dr Glazer propositioned you yet—or given you a fumble?'

The girl did not reply. It was as if she hadn't heard. She just stared, but as if she was not seeing anything.

'Oh, come on, sweetie,' said Christine. 'Did he or didn't he?'

It so happened that Glazer had propositioned the girl at the very first session and he had obtained no response.

'You are a virgin,' he told her, 'and part of your trouble is that your sex life has been too long delayed. If you delay it any longer the delay might cause irreparable harm. It is wrong for you not to have a sexual object in life and that sexual object should be intercourse with a member of the opposite sex. Perhaps you have not accomplished your natural sexual function because of fear, but you need have no fear with me. I am your doctor and it is obvious that your libido has been diverted and frustrated. If that frustration continues it could result in life-long insanity, and you don't want that, do you? I can help you to free your libido and fulfil the first function of womanhood. You want to be a woman, don't you?'

The girl hadn't replied. She just stared and when she felt him inserting his fingers between her knees, exerting pressure, she just stood up and walked to the door.

'Take her back to the ward,' said Glazer.

That was a week ago.

'Come on, sweetie,' Christine said, not unkindly. 'Snap out of it. You'll never get out of here unless you do. You've got a tongue in your head, haven't you?'

The girl didn't reply. She just stared.

Nurse Lois Summerton came into the ward. She put an arm around the girl's shoulders.

'Your parents are here to see you, Jacqueline,' she said softly.

Jacqueline didn't reply, but she stood up rigidly and walked towards the locked door, the nurse holding her lightly by the arm as she turned the key. When the door was closed behind them Christine jerked a nicotine-stained thumb.

'You wouldn't believe it,' she said. 'But that kid stabbed a man to death.'

'Well, I never!'

'You never can tell can you?'

'That's a fact, you can't.'

Raine and Veronica were waiting for Jacqueline in Dr Glazer's office.

As soon as she saw them Jacqueline cried out.

'Mummy! Daddy!'

She ran to them and hugged them both in turn. Raine put the back of his hand to his eyes.

Dr Glazer was delighted.

'You see!' he said, turning to Nurse Summerton. 'It worked, it worked!'

He beamed as a man might who had made some great scientific breakthrough, as if he personally had brought about some miraculous cure. He spread his arms wide like a *jongleur* on having successfully performed a difficult trick.

'Sit down, everybody, sit down,' he said. 'Nurse, can you arrange for a pot of tea? Good.'

He rubbed his hands, leaning forward and smiling at Jacqueline.

'Now, we're on speaking terms at last, are we, Jacqueline?'

Jacqueline did not reply.

'You may not realise it, Jacqueline,' Glazer continued, 'but since you were admitted here you have been in what we call a catatonic coma.'

'That surely was brought on by shock,' said Raine. 'That stupid judge—sending her for psychiatric treatment.'

Dr Glazer held up his hand.

'Please, Mr Raine. Do not belittle your own profession, I beg of you.'

What he also implied was Please, I beg of you, do not interrupt me. He put the tip of his fingers together in a way that reminded Raine of Dr Emrys Shiplake.

'The judge was not stupid. Far from it. Jacqueline does need treatment.

'Now, Jacqueline, now that I can get through to you I should explain that I invited your parents down here. Normally we do not permit visitors until two weeks have elapsed in order to allow the patient to settle down.

'However, in your case I found it imperative to get you out of your coma as quickly as possible.'

Nurse Lois Summerton brought in a tray of tea.

'So I invited your parents down—and lo!—we're on the first steps to recovery already.'

Jacqueline stared past him at the poplar trees in the drive, black and bereft of leaves. Raine followed her gaze. He remembered her walking under those trees one Sunday afternoon, turning to wave back at him.

'What I have found very useful in cases similar to yours, Jacqueline, is to get the family together and act out the problem, your problem.'

'She has no problem,' said Raine.

'Please, Mr Raine.'

Dr Glazer turned to Jacqueline again.

'Now, what I propose, Jacqueline, is that we all get together once a week, your mother and father, you and me, and talk this thing over and try to get you sorted out. You must admit you are a little confused, aren't you?'

Jacqueline made no reply.

'Dr Glazer,' said Raine. 'I suggest it is you who is confusing Jacqueline.'

'Mr Raine do you wish me to continue with treatment for your daughter or not?'

'I want to get her out of here, that's all.'

'You cannot take her out of here until she is officially pronounced cured, Mr Raine.'

Glazer turned to Veronica.

'Mrs Raine, you have said nothing so far. Are you willing to take part in this family therapy?'

'If it will help Jacqueline, yes.'

'Good. Even if only one parent is co-operative, that is a help.'

Dr Glazer took a cube of sugar and began to chew it, noisily. He waited until it had dissolved before he spoke again.

'Tea, Jacqueline?' Nurse Summerton asked.

Jacqueline did not reply. It was as if she had not heard the question.

'Tea, Mrs Raine?'

'Thank you, no sugar, thank you.'

'Tea, Mr Raine?'

'No, thank you.'

He was thinking of that afternoon at Brinstead Manor with the Women's Institute trio in flower petal hats. Glazer turned to Veronica again.

'Try to cast your mind back, Mrs Raine. Can you remember any other occasions when Jacqueline was violent?'

'Jacqueline was never violent!' Veronica protested.

'Not even as a child?'

'No.'

'Not even as a child? She never broke a doll or a toy?'

'Oh, well. Perhaps there were one or two occasions.'

'Can you remember them? Let's start at the beginning, shall we, Mrs Raine?'

Raine closed his eyes. No, the nightmare wasn't over.